BEHIND THE LIES

B. IVY WOODS

BRETAGEY PRESS

For Heather,
this project wouldn't have been completed without you!

CHAPTER 1

"Just a couple more things," Sean Barlow said as he typed on the keyboard in front of him. He looked at the query he just wrote that would finally give him access to all the data he needed. The screen illuminated his face, the only source of light in the entire office. Anyone else might have been frightened, alone in a sea of empty cubicles, but not him — this had become his norm.

Sean glanced at the time on the corner of the screen. "Dammit," he said to no one because there was no one to say it to. Another night spent at the Edmon Cybersecurities headquarters after everyone had already left for the day. He had hoped to be able to get home before the start of the latest Nationals baseball game, but that hope was dashed. He glanced at the baseball sitting in the case on his desk and thought that there was still a chance he might catch some of it, however.

It would have been helpful if someone developed the technology that would allow him to transport himself to the game and back within seconds. That would be super convenient right now so that he could at least get a glimpse of the game live. After all, it was 2098 for crying out loud.

He moved some papers around and placed them in his top drawer, planning to sort through them in a couple of days. He tried to keep his desk somewhat neat for appearances sake, so that everyone who walked by would have their attention drawn to the baseball on his desk. It was one of his most prized possessions because he caught it when his favorite player scored a home run four years ago. One of the things he was going to do with all of the money he was making from Edmon was buy season tickets to a box seat and he was getting closer and closer to that goal.

Speaking of that goal, Sean glanced to his right, before logging on to the server. The temptation to continue the search to find the Cyber Edge file was great, but he refrained. Stopping to see if he'd have any luck in finding it again would only further delay his initial timeline of getting home tonight further.

The work he'd done on the database would bring in more money than he could have ever thought of. There was also the potential to get even more money if he came forward with the name of the person who hired him. He was still deciding what to do about that.

Focusing back on his regular job, Sean clicked a button and watched as his computer ran a database query that would decide whether or not he left the office anytime soon. He tapped his foot a couple of times to the low humming noise the computer made as it started performing the updates he'd asked it to do.

A glance around the room confirmed he was alone, which one would expect at this time of night. Work had picked up even more in recent months, but he couldn't complain. His bank account had never looked better, but he rarely saw anyone in his personal life. It did make it easier to finish tasks up without having distractions, but not having much of a social life was hard. That was supposed to change tonight, but he'd cancelled at the last minute due to this falling into his lap. Life like this got quite lonely on occasion, but he knew he was doing the right thing for himself at this moment. This time commitment wouldn't last forever, and when he was on the other side of it, life would be so much better. Nothing was going to stop him from getting the job done.

It wouldn't surprise him if there were other people working this late at night. Whether you worked from home or in the office, Edmon culture pushed for you to be working for as long as it took to get the job done. Hell, he would have been at home as well, but he thought he could wrap up this last task quickly. Sadly, that hadn't been the case.

Curiosity got the best of him, and Sean decided he would go into the server that was assigned to him. It didn't take him any time to login. *Should he perform a search while he waited? What harm would it do?*

He started his search and as soon as it began he noticed that a file had been modified, dated as of two minutes ago. *Someone else was on this server? At this time of night?*

He grabbed his phone and held it up to his monitor. Just as he was about to press record, this person hopped on, then hopped off, making Sean further question what the point was. Sean didn't recognize their IP address in the quick second that he saw it, which was strange because he was only one of a handful of people who had access to this particular server. *Who was that?*

Sean shook the thoughts from his head, figuring that it was someone who might have been performing evening maintenance on the server. He leaned back in his chair and promised himself he would check on the test in a couple of minutes. All he needed was five minutes to close his eyes to rejuvenate his energy levels and his mood. Maybe he'd make it home in time for the fourth inning.

When a couple of minutes had passed and the computer was still running the query, Sean stood up and stretched. He walked over to look at the window closest to his cubicle. Darkness had fallen over Washington, D.C. The lack of light in the sky and the absence of cars on the street only amplified the stillness of his surroundings. In the back of his mind, he knew that the lack of traffic would make it easier to get home and catch whatever he could of the baseball game.

Those thoughts soon vanished, and shock overtook them.

Sean turned around to go back to his desk, and he jumped back. He could see a dark figure sitting in front of his computer. The person wore a baseball cap obscuring their face from view.

"Who are you? Why are you in my seat?"

The person looked up at him, and it felt as if they were staring into his soul. He could see the wild look in their eyes, and Sean recoiled in shock when he saw their face. He retreated further and put his hands up to defend himself. He didn't know what to expect and wanted to be prepared for anything. The person jumped out of the chair, and Sean took a step back. Maintaining some distance was key, but the person in the chair was faster. Quicker. More agile. The next thing Sean knew, a knife blade rapidly entered his torso. Sean's eyes widened, and his mouth fell open as the excruciating pain flowed through him. The assailant removed the knife and Sean's hands immediately went to clutch the open wound as blood flowed out no matter how much pressure he put on the cut. He wanted to groan in pain, but for some reason, he couldn't.

Sean tried to find the words to say, but none came out. *What had he done to deserve this?* He glanced at the exit and at the window. Could he make a run for it? There was no way he would be able to get out of the window without falling to his death from the eighth floor anyway.

"Nothing to say?" the voice asked. "Well, that's too bad." A sickly smile appeared on the person's face before he grabbed Sean by the hair.

"No," was the last word he uttered before his throat was slit. He tried to scream once more, but his body found it too difficult. As he fell, he knocked into his desk and he watched as the shadowy figure looked down on him. His prized baseball wobbled and fell to the ground just as he was stabbed once more.

CHAPTER 2

*N*aomi Porter closed her laptop with a decisive click before turning to her boyfriend, Reed Wright, with a smile on her face. "I'm finally done."

"About time. You've been working a lot of overtime these last few months."

"I have to do what I have to do to finish my work, Reed. And I'll admit, some of it has to do with needing a distraction. You know that and sometimes you have to do the same."

Reed's stare told her that he did, but she held her breath in case he wanted to continue. They'd had this same discussion over and over when Edmon constantly needed her to put in longer hours for them. As one of the biggest cybersecurity firms in the world, it came as no surprise that Edmon had Naomi working hard to make sure that their databases and servers were secure. Naomi worked for their headquarters in Washington D.C. as a developer. Her main project was extracting data in databases.

"We're already a couple innings into the game."

Naomi let out a sigh of relief because Reed wanted to

"

avoid the argument too. She regretted not being able to spend more time with him without their work coming in the way and that was what tonight was supposed to be. The biggest reason why she was watching the game was because he wanted to, and he got first choice tonight. Doug's request a couple of hours ago had almost thrown a wrench into their plans, but Naomi finished in record time.

"Looks like I missed more than just a couple of innings," Naomi said as she glanced at the TV. "The game is practically over."

"I didn't want to say that and make you feel bad." Reed reached for his beer on the table.

"Do you want another? I'm on my way to the kitchen to grab one anyway."

For a second, Reed looked shocked before he returned to his normally calm state. "Oh yeah, that'll be great."

After waiting for Reed to finish his beer, Naomi scooped up the empty bottle and took it to the kitchen for recycling. She quickly grabbed two more bottles from the fridge and returned to the living room, setting one on the table, before sitting next to Reed, one leg folded under her.

"Thanks," he said, gesturing to the beer. "Did you complete everything you needed to finish?"

Naomi sighed dramatically as she sunk further into the dark grey couch. "You know that my work at Edmon is never done."

"Well, did you at least get ahead on some of the things you needed to finish?" Reed cocked a brow before taking a pull from the bottle.

"Yes, I did, but I'm sure there will be things added to my plate tomorrow."

"And that's why I started my own business." Reed prided himself on his abilities as a private investigator. In fact, it was the reason they had met in the first place, when Naomi's mother had called him in after Paige Harris had been kidnapped.

"Makes sense. Sometimes, working for yourself has its advantages."

"I'm not going to say that there aren't any challenges — Oh shit!" Reed straightened abruptly as he watched a member of the opposing team hit a home run.

"Yikes," Naomi said before she put her own beer up to her lips. "Looks like I've jinxed the game by stopping work. Things are taking a turn for the worse."

Reed chuckled. "Tell me about it."

Naomi and Reed put their beers on the coffee table and he pulled her into his arms. Moments like this were treasured especially due to the very busy lives they led. Spending a quiet evening together was a treat because they were sometimes interrupted by Reed's workload, depending on if he was on a case and had to work all hours of the night, or Naomi's job which sometimes required her to spend longer hours in the office. But when they were in each other's presence, they focused on each other and their relationship, each knowing that despite work, this was their priority.

Reed tossed his head back, and it hit the wall behind them. "This game is over."

"Yeah, I hate to admit it, but that's what it's looking like."

"Are you tired?"

"No," Naomi said as a yawn escaped her lips. "However, I think my body is calling me a liar."

"Wouldn't be the first time."

Naomi attempted to hide a smile that was fighting to appear on her face. She knew he was referring to some of their adventures in the bedroom, but she wouldn't give him the pleasure of telling him that he was right.

"I'm not opposed to heading to bed early."

A yawn escaped a second time. "Looks like I'm not either. Let's do it."

Naomi had decided to stay over at Reed's that night. The couple tended to switch off when it came to staying at each other's places. Reed grabbed the remote, turned the television off and stood as Naomi stretched her limbs. Giving Naomi a helping hand, Reed tugged her into his arms, tightly hugging her before planting a lingering kiss on her lips.

"What was that for?"

Reed shrugged. "Just because."

"I'll take that." Naomi leaned up and kissed him back. "And that was me returning the favor."

Reed patted her on the butt, and the couple went their separate ways in order to make sure everything was shut down for the night before for climbing into bed. Naomi thought about reminding Reed if he actually purchased a Simon, it could do all of this for them. The automated system, which did many of the common tasks Naomi no longer had to think about, was a key feature in the apartment she and her best friend, Paige, had chosen to live in, and had made their lives so much easier. Reed, on the other hand, preferred to do the mundane tasks of everyday life and was determined not to have a Simon in his life.

It wasn't long before Naomi found herself laying on Reed's chest after he turned off the bedroom lights, his heartbeat lulling her into a peaceful sleep.

* * *

"WHAT?" Naomi mumbled as she was roused from the dream she was having. She heard a ringing in the background of what she thought was her subconsciousness, but as it continued, she realized she was hearing it in real time. *Is that Reed's phone?*

Her mind and body didn't feel well rested, and she was convinced that there was no way she had slept more than three hours. Naomi cracked open an eye and saw that Reed was still asleep. She gave him a gentle nudge. "Reed, your phone is ringing."

A groan came from the other side of the bed before she heard him fumbling for the device. A glimpse at her phone confirmed it was two in the morning. Who would be calling at this time of night? Naomi's thoughts weren't able to connect the dots, and she wondered if she could tune Reed out while he was on the phone and go back to sleep. Or he could take the call in another room. Either one was a viable option. Naomi reached over and turned on the lamp next to her side of the bed.

"Wright," he said when he answered the phone. Naomi wished she could hear what the person on the other end of the line was saying. Sensing this wouldn't be as quick as she hoped, Naomi stretched and walked to the bathroom. When she glanced at Reed as she was walking by, she noted how serious his expression was. When she finished, she opened the bathroom door and stood in the doorway. Reed was still on the phone, and it was easy to tell the conversation wasn't going well.

Naomi crawled back into bed and patiently waited for

Reed to get off the phone. A few minutes later, he hung up the phone, putting it down on the side table before running a hand through his brown hair.

"What's wrong?" Naomi asked as she placed a hand on his back. She hoped the gentle touch would offer him some comfort.

"There's been a murder. I've been called in to help."

That was the last thing Naomi expected him to say. "Oh no. That's horrible! Wait, the police need a private investigator to consult on a case?"

"Yeah…because that's not all."

Naomi held her breath. "What else is there?" She straightened, readying herself for whatever news he told her.

"It happened at the Edmon offices."

Naomi waited a beat. "You're kidding." That couldn't be right.

"I wish I were."

"Well, how the hell is anyone supposed to go to sleep after that?" A muted groan escaped her lips as she slumped back against the headboard, a thousand anxious thoughts fluttering through her head.

"I'm not sure but try to. I'm going to grab a quick shower and head out, but hopefully I'll be back soon." He swung his legs out from under the covers.

Almost as if the news had finally sunk in, Naomi grabbed his hand before he could fully get out of bed. "Wait, do you know who it is?"

Reed gave her fingers a gentle, reassuring squeeze and shook his head. "No, but as soon as I know something I'll let you know."

While Reed got ready, Naomi tried to get back to sleep,

but failed. She closed her eyes and tried meditating to see if that could help her, but no luck. In a huff, Naomi had rolled over to her other side, when Reed walked back into the bedroom.

"I'm going to head out."

Naomi sat up and opened her arms. "I'll see you when you get back."

"Hopefully, it won't be all night." He laid a kiss on her lips, walking out the bedroom one more time.

When Naomi heard the door close, she laid back on the bed and closed her eyes, wishing that once again she could fall back to sleep. As she predicted, Naomi couldn't fall back to sleep. Instead, she made some coffee and paced back and forth in the living room of Reed's condo. Cupping her hands around the mug, she savored a sip, proud that she didn't royally screw it up due to Reed's lack of technological conveniences.

What if the victim was someone she knew? Naomi debated reaching out to June Liu, a co-worker and friend, and Doug Jefferies, her boss, but refrained. Reed would have told her it was either of them. This wasn't public information yet, so it wasn't worth alarming them. But she wanted to talk to someone if they were awake. She grabbed her phone and studied the list of contacts. Her best bet was Paige, who might have been up late for work, but Naomi was also worried about telling her the news. After all, Paige had a bigger connection to the company now than most people did because her kidnapping was directly related to Edmon.

Naomi shifted her weight again, staring at the phone in her hand. She knew Paige would have wanted to know as soon as possible and would be hurt if Naomi kept something this big from her. With a heavy sigh, Naomi began to type.

Naomi: Are you awake?

She felt guilty as soon as she pressed 'send.' Chances were, if Paige was asleep, she would have muted her phone so she wouldn't be disturbed.

Paige: I actually just laid down in bed. What's up?

Naomi: Is it alright if I call you? If not, we can speak tomorrow.

Guilt tugged at Naomi again, and her mindset only shifted due to Paige's name popping up on her screen.

"Paige, I had a feeling you'd be up."

"Yeah, I was wrapping up some stuff for work. What's up?" Paige turned her camera on so they could see each other while they spoke. Her long blonde hair was up in a messy bun and not a speck of makeup could be found on her face. She yawned before she took a closer look at Naomi. "Are you crying? What's wrong? Where's Reed?"

"This stays here, okay? Well, I'm sure it will be all over the news at some point today, and you might want to warn your office that it's coming your way too." Edmon had offices in Virginia, too, and being how interconnected Virginia, Washington, D.C., and Maryland were, she was positive Senator George Butler of Virginia, Paige's boss, would want to make a statement about this.

"Woah, what is going on? You're rambling, and I can't keep up."

Naomi took a deep breath to try and center herself. Her behavior wasn't doing anything to keep the anxiousness she knew was raring and ready to come out from snapping. "I don't have much information yet, but there's been a murder the Edmon headquarters."

Paige's eyes became wide as she slowly blinked while she took in what Naomi said. Her mouth dropped open before her hands could cover it. She tried to say something, but her words came out muffled.

"I didn't get any of that."

"I said, you've got to be shitting me. Do you think it could be related to..." Paige let her words trail off, but Naomi knew what she was referring to.

"I don't know, but I won't say that thought didn't cross my mind. However, so far, the answer is we don't know. In fact, everything I just told you is all I know, and I only know this much because the call came in to Reed while I was here."

Paige didn't say anything after that, instead the expression on her face told me everything I needed to know. Fear shone through her eyes before she steeled herself, showcasing the armor she'd put in place after she'd survived everything my father and half-brother had inflicted on her.

When she didn't say anything, I continued, "Do you want some type of security? Maybe that would be wise to get some-one, given—"

"No, I don't think hiring security makes sense, at least right now. I think I want to know more about what's happening before we take any big steps. I'd like to let our chief of staff know about this, just so that she can properly prepare our boss for what might be occurring tomorrow."

"That's completely fine with me."

"But how are you? I can only imagine the mental toll it's taking on you too."

Naomi didn't know how to answer that. She looked down at her hands and licked her dry lips before she answered Paige's question. "Honestly, I'm in the same boat as you. I don't know how to react because we don't have that much information yet. Reed was called in to be a consultant on the case, and that was part of the reason why I called you so late. I have so many thoughts running through my head, it's somewhat hard to keep track and stop myself from freaking out."

"I get it, but also this could really have nothing to do with us. Your father is in jail, and your half-brother hasn't been seen or heard from since June near Baltimore."

"I know, but I just can't help but feel guilty."

"Stop it. None of this is your fault. The victim could have been killed for a number of reasons. It could've been random; it could've been an ex-lover out for revenge. Not saying any of those reasons are good, of course, but what I'm trying to say is none of this should make you feel guilty. We are all allowed to be upset and shaken but try to remove the guilt from your mind. It's only going to cause more stress and pain."

Naomi knew Paige was right, and having it come from someone who had lived through such a horrific ordeal was powerful. It still didn't stop the guilt she was feeling, because, without a doubt, Naomi knew the reason Paige had experienced what she did was because of their relationship. And Paige's words did little to soothe the mental anguish she felt.

$\mathscr{N}$aomi was sitting on the couch, passing the time on her computer because sleep wasn't coming any time soon. She'd done a couple of tasks that she had initially put off for tomorrow. Normally, between staring at a computer screen and the soothing grey tones in Reed's home would ease her tired mind and help calm her anxiousness, but there was no chance of that now.

It had been a few hours since Reed had left and he hadn't called or texted, but she hadn't been expecting to hear from him either. With that in mind, it still didn't cure Naomi's thoughts about the situation nor ease her mind about what was happening and about how much she didn't know.

When she heard the lock on the front door disengage, she jumped slightly as her heart rate picked up, but she kept herself from rushing to the door. The soft light from the lamp in the living room showed off the weary lines that had settled on Reed's face as he entered the room and came closer to her.

"Can I get you anything?" Naomi asked. She checked the time, making a small note of the early morning hour, and closed her laptop. She slid it off her lap onto the coffee table and prepared to stand. Flashes of when his face last looked like this, during his recovery after he got hurt trying to save Paige from Naomi's father, fluttered through her memory. Naomi had hoped she would never see this look on his face again, but here it was. She felt for him because she could only imagine what it was like to view a murder scene.

"No, no. You should probably sit while I tell you this."

Naomi slowly sat back down, and Reed joined her after he dropped his bag near one end of the couch. When he was seated, he reached over, grabbed her hand, and rubbed small circles on the back with his index finger. His actions did little to calm her nerves. *What was he about to tell her?* He took a deep breath before he looked her in the eyes, his blue ones clashing with her brown ones, setting her nerves abuzz. For a moment, it was just the two of them, staring at each other as he reached over to tuck a piece of her dark curly-coily hair behind her ear. His touch brought a warmth she feared would grow cold once he had delivered the news he was set to give.

"Have I ever told you that one of the reasons why I decided to leave MPD and do my own thing was because I hated being the person who had to tell a family their loved one had died?"

Naomi shook her head. He didn't talk much about his time as a police officer. She rubbed a hand down his back, trying to comfort him before he told her what happened.

"The victim was named Sean Barlow. He was a programmer at Edmon, just like you. Did you know him?"

Naomi tossed the name around in her head before she said, "The name sounds familiar, but he wasn't on my team. There are so many divisions within Edmon headquarters, nationwide, and internationally, that it's hard to keep track unless you see the person on a regular basis."

"Understandable, and we confirmed that he wasn't, but didn't know if you knew him since you were both programmers."

Naomi let out a breath. She regretted feeling a sense of relief it wasn't someone she knew. She still felt terrible for Sean and his family. "How was he killed?"

"Stabbed in the abdomen and his throat was slit. The crime scene was pretty gruesome, and I'll leave out the nitty gritty details, unless that's something you want to hear. Even his autographed baseball got caught in the bloodshed. It was found a few feet away from him, covered in blood. We're pretty sure it was done with the knife that was left at the scene of the crime."

Naomi did a double take. "Wait, the suspected weapon was left behind?"

Reed nodded. "Preliminary scans showed the suspect didn't leave any evidence that could be linked to who they are, but more tests will need to be done once the knife is taken back to the station."

"Is that normal? For the murderer to leave the murder weapon behind?"

"Depends on the situation. I think it's weird here because the suspect had plenty of time to get away as far as we know, so why leave it? If we find anything that disputes that, I'll change my opinion."

"Any motive?"

Reed shook his head. "So far nothing, but we'll find out more as we dig into the victim's background. Find out more about who he was, who he associated with, and things like that. Edmon will be releasing a press statement shortly and will be providing counseling to those who need it."

"That's good. I'm definitely going to schedule an appointment with my doctor about it." She knew being proactive about what might cause her anxiety to increase was key in trying to keep it at bay. "How did the suspect get past security to kill Sean? Security at Edmon is tight and has grown tighter ever since my father—"

Reed brought her hand up to his lips and gave it a kiss. The gesture, although small, made her feel safe, giving the turmoil that surrounded them. "It's okay. All signs are pointing to a hacking that essentially caused Edmon's security system to freeze for a few seconds, allowing whoever this was to get through without detection. I'm waiting on images from MPD during the time we suspect the break-in happened."

"Okay, it sounds like they knew what they were doing and potentially had been inside of Edmon before. I don't know if the layout of Edmon is available anywhere. Then again, you can find just about anything on the internet, if you try hard enough."

Reed waited a beat before he said, "I'm glad you mentioned that, Naomi, because you aren't safe at Edmon right now. It's not a good idea for you to be going into the office at the moment."

And there it was. At that moment, she felt like she was passing through a hailstorm with no way to escape.

"But, as far as we know, he's not connected to me." Her protest sounded feeble, even to her own ears.

"That's true. Police Chief Mark Hughes has already spoken to Wilson Billings, the CEO of Edmon, to tell him everything the Metropolitan Police Department knows so that steps forward can be discussed. I assume one of the items would be whether or not employees should return to the office and in what capacity. Given everything that has gone on in your life the last few months, I would think working from home or from here are your best options."

Deep down, Naomi knew he was right, but she wasn't going to let some unknown entity scare her into hiding. "I'll think about it, okay? And discuss it with Doug to make sure he agrees." Doug, Naomi's boss, knew about some of the trauma she'd gone through just a few months prior and she thought that would make their conversation easier.

"Okay, and there is something I wanted to ask you."

"Oh?"

"How would you feel about helping me with this case?"

Naomi stared at Reed for a moment, contemplating about if he was being serious. "For real?"

"Yes." Reed's expression lightened and that made her feel more at ease. "We worked well together when it came to finding Paige. Having someone who knows more about Edmon than anything would help eliminate any connection that this is related to them."

"Or confirm there is one," Naomi added, off-hand.

Reed's brow rose. "Do you think there might be one?"

Naomi shrugged. "This is the second incident at Edmon in recent months. Wouldn't it be reasonable to assume there's a connection?"

"Could be. I would rather have evidence that shows the relationship between the two first."

"I can understand that." Seeing that he was already starting to act like they were working the case together, Naomi smiled at his enthusiasm, trying to hide her own apprehension.

"Nonetheless, I need to think about it and clear it through the appropriate channels."

"It's already being worked on in case you agreed. Chief Hughes thought the same thing after I brought it up and mentioned that there was no time to waste."

Naomi thought about when they had gathered to meet at the hospital to check on Reed after her father's arrest, and Chief Hughes had mentioned her potentially working in this field. She wasn't sure if this was quite what he had in mind.

CHAPTER 4

*E*dmon Media Advisory

Washington, D.C., Edmon CEO, Wilson Billings, to all Edmon employees:

Dear Team Edmon,

It is with deep regret that I share with you the news of the death of Sean Barlow. We have lost a pinnacle part of our community due to the selfish acts of others. A police investigation is in progress to find out what transpired in the hours leading up to and after Sean's death. There will be an event to celebrate Sean's life that will be taking place in the very near future. If you need any help or guidance during this terrible time, please feel free to reach out to your HR representative. If you want to share any thoughts, memories, or condolences about Sean to his family, there will be a special email account and a station set up in our lobby for you to leave things, if you choose to do so.

We will continue to pay tribute to Sean in the best way we know how by continuing his work at Edmon and to push forth under these difficult circumstances.

Wilson Billings

"Well, that wasn't too bad, especially for a statement that had to navigate someone dying from unnatural causes," Naomi mumbled to herself as she read the advisory again. How horrible it was that Sean's family had to go through this took over all the thoughts in her mind. At the very least, she was happy that an adequate announcement had been made and the rest of her coworkers and team were finding out about the news and that she could now freely talk to them about what happened.

Although Edmon was huge, Naomi interacted with Wilson on a regular basis in recent months. One of the projects that she was working on required her to report to him directly, but Doug was still her direct manager.

A ping on Naomi's computer signaled the receipt of another email. This one was from Doug, requesting a virtual team meeting in one hour. It gave her just enough time to pull herself together and make it look like she had gotten more than just a few hours of sleep after last night's events. Naomi had just finished putting on some light makeup to cover up the lingering bags under her eyes when Reed walked into the bathroom.

"What's going on?"

"Doug is calling an all-team meeting to what I assume will be a discussion about what happened to Sean and what our work lives will look like moving forward."

Reed nodded. "Hopefully, the recommendation would be that everyone will be working from home until further notice."

"I assume that would be one of the recommendations,

given that the building is still an active crime scene. I wonder if they'll allow people to go into the building to get their things."

"Employees are allowed to get their things, but they need to be escorted. There might be different provisions for the floor where Sean's cubicle is located. Do you have anything to get?" He frowned, as if simply being in the building would potentially put her in harm's way.

Naomi shook her head. "Whatever I need, I have here or at my apartment. Since I've been working late hours, I wanted to make sure that I had everything I needed to be able to work remotely."

Reed angled his body toward her. "Good. Naomi, it is clear one of the biggest cybersecurity firms in the world cannot protect its employees right now. While we don't know for sure Sean was targeted due to where he worked, there is a strong chance that was the case."

"And we have an infrastructure in place to stop this kind of thing, yet this was allowed to happen. I just feel a sense of déjà vu all over again." Naomi rubbed her arm after goosebumps appeared.

"Completely understandable. But just try not to go down that rabbit hole until we know more. I know that's easier said than done."

Naomi's lips twitched. He knew her all too well. "I need to get ready for this meeting, but we can chat after, if you want?"

Reed's eyes darted to the right as he tried to recall something. "Chief Hughes is supposed to call me in a few minutes, so I might have an update for you. I also don't know when the call will end, so you might be done before me."

"That's fine. I'll see you in a little bit." Naomi reached out and kissed Reed.

His hands moved and softly landed on either side of her face, giving him more control, and turning the kiss into one that was more sensual. She moved her head back slightly.

"I really have to go," she whispered.

"Ok." His hands fell to the side as she walked past him headed to the living room.

With just a few minutes to spare, Naomi was waiting for the team meeting to begin. A minute before the meeting was set to start, a coworker started the virtual meeting room and she patiently waited for Doug to start speaking.

"Good morning, everyone. As I'm sure most of you have heard, Sean Barlow, a coworker and friend to us, was killed last night at the Edmon D.C. office last night. If you haven't got a chance to read the note Wilson sent out to the whole company, I would suggest you do so. If you need to take personal time, please chat with me to let me know. If you need help getting through this or just want to talk to someone, Edmon has professionals at your service. Please let your HR representative know, and if you don't feel comfortable talking to them, feel free to come to me, and I will do my best to help you in your search."

Naomi watched as each of her coworkers listened to the words Doug was saying, and the somber looks on their faces spoke volumes. Doug continued to relay a similar message and tone to the email that Wilson had sent out to the entire company.

"And for the time being, our team will be going completely remote, so if you have any questions about that, feel free to send me a message about that too. If it's something I need to share with everyone else, I'll do so. Everyone should be hyper-vigilant about being on their laptops and checking their emails and messages, especially during work hours. If you need anything, don't hesitate to ask. Are there any questions?"

All of her coworkers shook their heads, but several of them were either crying or on the verge of tears. Who knew really what to ask during a time like this?

Hearing none, he said, "Then we'll operate as close to normal as possible, with the caveat that if you need extra help, please let us all know, and I'll let you know if anything changes. Thank you for hopping on today, and please don't hesitate to let me know if you need anything."

With that, the meeting ended, and Naomi was left staring at her laptop screen. Reed's proposal about her teaming up with him drifted back to the front of her mind. Taking the time off was something she would need to talk to Doug about. After a quick debate with herself, she pulled up Edmon's messenger and sent a quick message to Doug requesting a one-on-one meeting with him. She wasn't shocked to receive a calendar invite back almost immediately requesting they meet within the next ten minutes. That was enough time for Naomi to go and check to see if Reed was off the phone and grab a glass of water.

Naomi pushed her laptop to the side and got up. She walked down the hall and saw that Reed's door was still closed. Figuring that meant he was still speaking to Chief Hughes in the meeting, she walked back the way she came, this time detouring to the kitchen.

It wasn't long after she sat down again that Doug called. "Naomi, hi. How is everything going with you outside of...well, you know."

"Not too bad, given the circumstances that we are currently in." The lie fell from Naomi's lips with ease. Her mind was telling her things might get a whole lot worse, but she didn't know if that was her intuition talking or her anxiety.

"Is there anything I can do to help you?"

"Sort of." Naomi thought for a second about how to phrase what she wanted to say. "I assume that Edmon has no problem with any of its employees talking to the police?"

"Of course not. We want to cooperate to the full extent of our abilities so we can find out who did this to Sean."

"That's good to know. I assume they will be interviewing employees anyway. Switching topics a bit, if I want to take some time, would that be okay?"

"Of course. The policy I mentioned on our call a few minutes ago is open to everyone. Take as much time as you need. Did you know Sean?"

"I didn't. The name sounds familiar, but I don't think we were personally introduced to one another which, given the size of Edmon, isn't unbelievable." She paused for a moment, taking a second to collect her thoughts. "I just can't believe all this happened."

"Yeah, I'm having a hard time wrapping my head around everything that's going on as well. The next few hours and days will be interesting, for lack of a better word, but we will all make it through this."

"I do hope so."

Doug cleared his throat. "If you do you want to take that time off officially, please let me know, and I'll get it squared away on our end. Don't worry about how much time you want to take, but I will do check-ins periodically just to make sure you're okay and see when you plan on returning."

"Sounds good. I'll be in touch."

"Naomi, take care of yourself. You've been through a lot over the past few months. I'm going to check in on June as well to see how she is handling the news."

Naomi told herself that she would do the same. After the ordeal June had gone through just a few short months ago, it didn't hurt to reach out to make sure she knew she had a shoulder to lean on during this time. "Thank you so much, Doug, for chatting with me quickly."

"Not a problem. Talk to you soon."

Doug signed off, and Naomi closed her laptop, deciding that even looking at an email from work right now was too much for her to bear.

Working with Reed seemed to be a viable option at this point, although Naomi still had reservations. But deep down, she knew at, the very least, she'd take the time off to focus on her mental health. Just as she came to that conclusion, Naomi heard a door open and knew Reed just finished his call with Chief Hughes.

"Anything new to report?" she asked as Reed walked into the room.

"Not much. The investigation is continuing, and when they have more information, they'll send it my way and vice versa. How did your call go?"

"Well. Both the team meeting and my one-on-one with Doug were good. He gave me the option for taking time off, which I probably will take."

"I think that's a great idea."

There was a lingering question in his voice, and Naomi

knew it was probably connected to her joining him in this investigation, but he didn't say anything else. However, she knew once she'd confirmed her time off with Doug, she wouldn't have anything else holding her back, outside of her own thoughts and insecurities.

CHAPTER 5

"Thank you so much for meeting with me so quickly. I know that this was a last-minute thing."

"You know me. I told you if you need to make an emergency appointment, I will do my best to accommodate. What did you want to discuss today?"

The next day back in her own apartment, Naomi looked at Dr. Elise Evans. It wasn't surprising that the woman in front of her was the picture of professional perfection with her dark hair that had wisps of gray in it falling down on her shoulders, a white blouse, and a small pearl necklace. Whereas Naomi felt as if her world was spinning out of control. She thought the words would have just fallen out of her mouth, but she was having a hard time putting her thoughts together. "There was another incident at Edmon."

Dr. Evans tilted her head. "What type of incident?"

"Someone was murdered."

The gasp Dr. Evans let out was how Naomi had felt when she'd first found out. Naomi reiterated the details of the case that she knew so far, while Dr. Evans sat back and took notes.

"That is horrible. Are you overanalyzing and trying to find any links between Sean's murder and Paige's disappearance?"

Naomi shouldn't have been shocked that Dr. Evans was immediately able to draw the connection. After all, she was a professional, and Naomi had been a patient of hers for quite a while.

"I assume all of this is making you more anxious than normal as well."

Naomi nodded at the obvious deduction. "Definitely. It also doesn't help that I've been under a lot of stress in general trying to cope with the increased workload at Edmon and still trying to process my feelings about everything that happened with my father."

"How has that been going since the last time we spoke?" Dr. Evans' even tone emanated from the video call.

"Honestly, I feel as if this had happened, say, a year or two ago, I would have needed medical intervention. The weight I feel on my shoulders is heavy, but I think I've crumbled under less before, so when it comes to that, I think I'm doing much better. I'm in a better place." Maybe the more she said the words, the truer they would become in her own mind. Still, she had made immense progress in her mental health, and that was something to be proud of.

"Well, sometimes we can't control anxiety, no matter what measures we are taking to do so, but I know that you and I will do our best to keep everything under control. But if something does happen, I don't want you to beat yourself up over it."

Naomi swallowed hard. "That's easier said than done."

"Of course. I'm throwing it out there now in hopes if you do end up getting into that headspace, you remember that.

Switching gears here, how is everything going with your mother and step-father? And Reed?"

Naomi wiped her fingers over her eyes. When she lowered her hand, she blinked a couple of times as she prepared to share the other thing that had been on her mind. "Good! Everything is quiet with Mom and Logan. I need to make time to visit them. And things are going well with Reed. We've been spending a lot of time together. He also got called into help with the murder at Edmon. In fact, he asked me if I wanted to help him with the case."

"How do you feel about that?"

"I'm happy that he asked me to help him and that he thinks we make a great team. I assume my knowledge of Edmon is an added bonus."

"What are you afraid of?"

"Afraid of?" Naomi hadn't thought about it that way, but it was as if Dr. Evans had homed in on the true reason for her hesitation. She took a moment before she said, "I'm afraid of getting overwhelmed to the point where I just want to fall into bed and never leave. I'm afraid of failing everyone who would be depending on me if I were to help Reed. Most importantly, I'm afraid of hating myself if I do find out I'm connected to this in any way."

"So, this is stemming from the hatred you've felt as a result of finding out about your father's involvement in Paige's kidnapping?"

Naomi's eyes glazed over as Dr. Evans spoke, but Naomi knew she was telling the truth. "Yes. Yes, it is."

"Maybe joining this investigation with Reed would give you some closure. Then you can try to put it behind you. This doesn't mean forget it, but you have to find it in yourself to forgive yourself and understand none of this was your fault. It might also help your relationship grow stronger."

A tear fell from her eye that she hastily wiped away. "I know, you're right. Doesn't make it any easier to hear."

Empathy shone from Dr. Evans' eyes. "All of this is a lot for several people to be dealing with, let alone one person. And you're handling it well. Please remember that."

Her words made Naomi choke up, even though she tried to hold it together.

Naomi and Dr. Evans spoke for a few more minutes before Dr. Evans mentioned the session was almost over. She threw out a date and time for next week, and Naomi happily accepted.

When Naomi ended the video call, she reached over, grabbed her phone, and found a message from Paige.

Paige: Are you free tonight?

Naomi: Sure, what do you have in mind?

Paige: I was thinking we could do dinner and a movie? I should be home in a couple of hours.

Naomi smiled. They hadn't done that in a while.

Naomi: Sounds wonderful. Do you know what you want to eat?

Paige: I've had a taste for chicken stroganoff. I can run to the grocery store if we don't have all of the ingredients for it.

Naomi: Okay. I'll check with Simon to see what we have here, and I'll send you a list of things we need, if we need anything.

With that, she closed her laptop and went into the kitchen to start preparing for their girls' night in.

* * *

"THIS SMELLS SO GOOD," Paige said as the aroma from the food they were cooking spread throughout the kitchen area.

The warming smells provided a sense of comfort to Naomi while she poured a glass of wine. True to her words, Paige arrived home, and she and Naomi set off to cook their dinner for the evening.

"My stomach is growling, and my mouth is salivating at all these delicious smells. It might not be a bad idea to take our dinner out to the balcony if you didn't want to eat while the movie was on." Naomi took a sip of the wine and closed her eyes. The heady, robust flavor hit the spot, sending a delightful warmth through her limbs.

"That's a good idea. How was your day?"

Paige leaned a hip against the kitchen counter, sampling the wine from her own glass. "Not too bad. We are predominantly dealing with the aftermath of the murder at the Edmon building. And, of course, trying to represent our constituents in Congress. As to be expected, the murder has been dominating the news on and off the Hill."

Naomi knew Paige was right. No matter what station she turned to, Naomi could almost guarantee she would find something related to murder. The story had made national news, and everyone was clamoring to find out the latest details about the investigation.

"How about you? How are things at work?" She turned her attention back to the food.

"Well, right now, I'm going on vacation." Naomi quickly averted her eyes.

Paige dropped the dish towel she'd just snatched off the counter and turned to look at her best friend. "You're going to take leave? And you're not being forced to?" she asked, clearly not believing the words that had come out of Naomi's mouth.

"I did. I needed some time to just think for a little bit. I officially put my notice in yesterday. I'll be working tomorrow, and then that'll be it."

"Wow," Paige said. "I mean, I get it. I took a significant amount of time off, as you know. And even now, I'm still a little weary about going through my normal day-to-day life and pretending that everything is fine, so I understand. You hopped back into working almost right after...everything happened."

Naomi put the wine glass down, resting a hand on her friend's shoulder. "I don't know exactly how you feel, because I didn't live through being kidnapped, but there's been so much pressure on everyone attempting to act like everything is fine, and we aren't. We've both been completely changed by the experience, and that's okay."

Paige sighed. "I know, and I must say, being back at work and doing what I love helps me forget about all the other bullshit, somewhat."

"I can see that, and that used to be how I felt about my work with Edmon, but between what happened to you and now this murder, I almost feel as if Edmon is tainted. So, I thought the best thing I could do was have some time off, and it would do me a bit of good. Also Reed made a proposal—"

Paige jumped back and gasped. "Reed proposed to you?"

Naomi chuckled and squeezed Paige's shoulder. "No, I said he made a proposal to me. I could have chosen better wording there. Anyway, he asked if I would be willing to work with him on this murder investigation. I think I mentioned before he was asked to help MPD, and it wouldn't hurt to have someone who knows Edmon inside and out pretty well on the team. I think I'm going to do it."

"That's taking on a lot, but I'm proud of you, if you decided to do it."

Naomi nodded, before she turned to stir the chicken stroganoff. "I want to help however I can and having this vacation time would give me the chance to do it. I think it will help me not only find out the monster who did this, but also help me sort through my feelings on…well, everything."

"Great. Plus, you'll have all the inside information about where things stand."

Naomi snorted. "Potentially. But I don't know how much I'll be able to share, but I will share what I can. I plan on sharing it with Reed when he comes over later."

"Have you heard anything else about where the investigation is?"

Naomi shook her head and checked the clock before her phone pinged.

Reed: I'm going to be over later than I originally planned. Got tied up into something at the station.

Naomi: We can just see each other tomorrow.

Reed: Nope. I want you in my arms tonight.

Naomi smiled before she put her phone back down.

"Did he just text you?"

Naomi looked at Paige. "How'd you know?"

"The smile on your face." Paige nudged her with a giggle.

Grinning wider, Naomi couldn't deny that. She'd thrown out the suggestion of him going back to his own place tonight but hadn't actually wanted him to do that. She was happy he wasn't.

"Yeah, he should be over later tonight, apparently. Something came up at the police station. Maybe it has something to do with Sean's case." Naomi sighed. "I want to know more about where the case stands before I officially tell him that I want in."

* * *

LATER THAT EVENING, Naomi was lying in bed reading a book when she felt her phone vibrate on a bed.

Reed: *I'm here.*

She didn't bother responding. Instead, she threw the covers off of her body and left her bedroom. Her movie night had ended about an hour ago after both women decided the movie they were watching wasn't going to get any better, and she'd been waiting to hear from Reed since she had gone to bed.

Naomi walked into the hallway and flicked the light on. She moved to the front door and saw there was a small red light on a security system that had been installed after Paige was rescued. With a few clicks, Naomi was able to verify Reed had shown his ID, and a current screenshot of his face had matched. To double check, she looked at the small monitor near the door and found Reed standing on the other side of the door. Naomi unlocked the door and swung it open.

"Hey," she said.

Reed looked up and gave her a small smile. "Hey yourself," he said. He pulled her into his arms, somewhat awkwardly, given the small bag he was holding. He backed her into the apartment and closed the door with his foot before giving her a kiss.

"Why does it feel like it's been days since we've seen each other?" she asked.

Reed chuckled. "Because you've missed me that much."

Naomi rolled her eyes and playfully tapped him on the shoulder. "As if you didn't miss me."

"I didn't say I didn't," he replied, and the couple made their way into Naomi's bedroom. "Is it alright if I take a quick shower before we go to bed?"

"Sure, as long as you don't mind us talking after your shower."

"My shower might take longer than usual. I forgot you had a television in there."

Naomi smiled and shook her head. "Don't get lost in the baseball game too much while you're in there or you might turn into a prune."

"No promises, and won't one of your skincare products prevent that from happening? I'm happy to turn into a prune if it means that the Nats are going to win the game."

Naomi rolled her eyes. "You should tell Simon thank you because you'll have to use him to turn the television on and—"

Reed paused for a moment and looked at Naomi. "What's wrong?"

"I just remembered how big of a Nats fan Sean supposedly was."

Reed gave Naomi a sad smile before leaning over to give her hand a small squeeze before walking away.

He went over to the drawer that she had cleared out to give him space to keep a few items of clothing at her apartment just in case he spent the night. She'd started doing the same, and one shirt morphed into two t-shirts, which then morphed into several shirts and other items of clothing.

When he entered the bathroom, Naomi debated walking into the bathroom and telling him what she wanted to tell him while he was in the shower but refrained. He deserved some time to unwind and de-stress before she talked to him about what had been on her mind.

She returned to bed and opened the book she was reading before Reed showed up at her door. She read a few pages while she waited for the shower to stop running. When he'd exited the bathroom, billows of steam surrounded him. Naomi took her time staring at his muscular form without shame. With just a towel tied around his waist, Reed looked as if he had just stepped out of a magazine. He dropped the towel and gave her a little smirk, as he put on his boxer briefs and pajama pants.

"See something you like?"

"Yes. That might be the silliest question of all time," she said as he walked around to her side of the bed and sat down on the edge.

He leaned over and planted another kiss on her mouth. His lips on hers sent a tremble through her. The kiss grew more intense, and Naomi groaned when he pulled away. He licked his lips.

"Wait, what? Why'd you stop?"

"Because you wanted to talk. What's on your mind?"

"I want to talk to you about the suggestion you made about us working together to solve Sean Barlow's murder."

He crawled over Naomi to lay on the other side of the bed. She giggled as she placed the book on the night stand and slid deeper under the covers before turning to face him.

"I want to help you solve the case. I mean, I'm not a private investigator, but I do know Edmon, so I hope I can provide some assistance."

"I'd appreciate your assistance in other areas as well." Reed's hand skimmed over her hip and teased the skin at her lower back.

His lips landed on Naomi's before making their way to her jaw line. Soft kisses littered her skin before he made his way down her neck.

"Reed," Naomi said with a giggle. "I'm trying to be serious."

"Me too," he said and placed a kiss on her neck.

"I still have one more day at Edmon before I'm officially on vacation, so I can start helping you after that." She squirmed a bit in his arms.

Reed made a humming noise against her neck as he continued his assault.

Naomi spoke again. "You know, this means that we'll be spending a lot of time together, right?"

"Yep."

His short answers told her all that she needed to know. Naomi gently put her hands on his chest and pushed. He looked down at her, and his eyes told her he had other more important things to be worried about right now.

"What's up?"

"I just want to tell you I love you," she said.

"And I love you." He smiled warmly, before drawing her deeper down into the sheets. It wasn't long until all her anxieties drifted to the back of her mind.

CHAPTER 6

"I'm so glad you were able to join us."

Naomi smiled and folded her hands on her lap. She was still stunned because she was sitting in Chief Mark Hughes's personal office. The office was built to be a techie's dream. It shouldn't come as a surprise that the chief of police had the latest technology in his office space. From his computer — that she knew had to be worth tens of thousands of dollars — to his phone and the electronic map of Washington, D.C., which hung on his wall. Everything was the latest and greatest; some things even Naomi hadn't heard of. Surrounding all of the best technology the world had to offer were accolades upon accolades.

Awards lined the walls, showcasing the achievements Chief Hughes had made throughout his career. It was no wonder why he had reached the position that he was in, and yet, here he was taking time out of his busy day to talk to the two of them.

"As I'm sure you've seen, the Sean Barlow investigation has taken on a life of its own, in terms of what is being reported in the news." Chief Hughes pointed to the front page of a newspaper that showed a professional photo of Sean. If she had thought the case was big before, it was enormous now. Over the last couple of days, media outlets were throwing around conspiracy ideas about who might have killed Sean and what their motive might have been. There were also questions about whether or not there would be more murders and if this was the work of a serial killer. Naomi only tried to keep up with some of it, but there were certain points where even she had to turn the reports off because of how much it was getting to her.

"We need to wrap this investigation up as quickly as possible. Justice needs to be given to the Barlow family, and we don't want the general public to get even more worried and excited about this case than they already are. We've had reports of groups trying to take matters into their own hands, and as a public safety concern, that's the last thing we want to happen."

Naomi and Reed agreed before Reed spoke. "Have you discovered anything else that could point us into the direction of who might have done this?"

"We've dug into Sean's background, and as far as we can see, he's completely clean. He moved here to go to college, and after he graduated, he never left. His family lives in Florida and are heartbroken over his death." Chief Hughes paused and took a deep breath. "I couldn't imagine having to bury a child. My heart goes out to them."

Naomi's eyes drifted away from the Chief to look at one of the photos on his wall. There he stood with who she assumed was his wife and two children, as he was being sworn in as police chief. She knew he was more than likely thinking about his own kids.

"Edmon has been cooperating with the investigation and handed over this security footage from that night. Since Sean's estimated time of death was around 8:35 p.m., give or take a couple of minutes, we gathered footage from rush hour until about 9:30 p.m., just in case, his killer lingered around for a while. We're going through all the footage, but we figured this was a good place to start. Simon, play the security clips from the Barlow case."

"See, even he has a Simon," Naomi whispered to Reed.

Reed didn't respond, but soon the security footage filled the silence. Everyone's eyes were glued to the screen as people moving in and out of the building circulated on the screen. Naomi's eyes were glued to the screen until something caught her eye. She ran the scene through her head again before she spoke.

"Wait a minute. Can you go back twenty seconds?"

Chief Hughes looked at her. "What's wrong? What did you see? Simon, please rewind the video by twenty seconds."

Simon did as he was asked, and when it came to the section she wanted to talk about, she asked Simon to pause the video. The video showed a perfectly clear picture of the entrance outside of Edmon's headquarters.

"There is a person in a technician uniform right there."

"What's wrong with that?" Reed asked.

"They wouldn't be there that late, and if they were, they'd be leaving, not coming into the building."

"But you work at all hours of the day. You don't have contractors who come in after hours?"

Naomi shook her head. "When Edmon uses outside sources, we try to do so during the day. Edmon has no problem with us employees working late hours, but they try to keep contractors around only during the day. It can be a pain in the ass to let a non-employee into the building after hours, which starts at 6:30 p.m. Timestamp says that it's 7:33 p.m. there. I would definitely look over who signed in or used an Edmon badge to enter at that time. Reed also said that there was some suspicion that someone hacked the security system and I agree."

Chief Hughes stroked his chin and said, "I'm not sure how quickly we would have known this information if you hadn't said anything."

That made Naomi proud, and Reed reached over to squeeze her hand. Maybe joining in on this investigation would be worth it after all.

"Let me see if I can get the sign-in records for the night of the murder. Simon, please call Kelly and have her grab the login data from Edmon for the Sean Barlow case."

A beep was heard before a chirpy voice came through the speaker on the police chief's desk. "Sir, I just sent the login data from the Barlow case to your screen. It should be appearing right now."

As soon as she said that, the sign-in logs appeared on the big screen television located on the police chief's wall.

"Detective Finley should be coming in shortly."

"Thank you, Kelly."

Naomi scanned it quickly and didn't find anything that showed a guest or an employee entering the building the same time this person entered Edmon headquarters. She sank back onto her heels and looked over at Reed, and he was already looking at her.

"No one signed in at that time, which means they overrode the security system some type of way," Naomi said, and both Chief Hughes and Reed agreed.

Kelly's warning was perfectly timed because there was a knock on the door. When Chief Hughes gave his permission, a man in what looked to be in his early-to-mid thirties strolled into the room.

Reed stood up to shake his hand. "Sam Finley."

"Reed Wright," the newcomer answered back. "Haven't seen you in a while."

Naomi looked between the two men, trying to figure out the connection between the pair, but was at a loss. Had they worked together?

Chief Hughes shook the detective's hand as well before Detective Finley's eyes landed on Naomi.

"And who would you be?"

"Naomi Porter," she said as she stood up. He held out his hand, and she shook it while giving him a polite smile.

Reed moved closer to her and announced, "She's helping with the case. Is this your case?"

Detective Finley nodded. "I am. Detective Olson was reassigned." He looked over at the television screen. "I see you have the login information from the day of the murder."

"Naomi made a pretty big discovery, and we were just about to look through the guestbook to see if anything seemed amiss," Chief Hughes answered for the group.

Detective Finley raised an eyebrow at Naomi. "Oh really? What did you find?"

Naomi turned to Chief Hughes. "If I may?"

He nodded, and Naomi took center stage.

"Simon, please switch back to the previous screen."

The monitor flipped back to the surveillance video from the night of Sean Barlow's murder. Naomi found the section she was looking for and asked Simon to play the video again. When the video played for several seconds, Naomi took a step forward and paused the video.

She pointed at the figure on the screen but avoided touching it. "As I mentioned just before you got here, there is no way a technician from Technological Mechanics, if you go by the piece of the emblem that we can see, would have been on Edmon's property at 7:30 p.m. that night. It's not allowed unless there's an absolute meltdown and no one on staff can fix it. A lot of our technical issues are handled in-house, because over the years as Edmon grew, the company absorbed other companies and added technicians to our staff, so we've essentially become self-sustaining."

Naomi watched as each man in the room digested the news she just shared. No one spoke for a moment, and her comment hung in the air.

Detective Finley took a step forward. "If what you're saying is true, how were they able to override the security system of the biggest cyber security firm in the world. We need more information from Edmon."

Naomi wondered what type of technology that individual must have in order to be able to override Edmon's security system. They must have a lot of money or is working for someone who does.

"There is also the possibility that someone who was already in the building let them in," Reed said as he put his hand on the small of her back.

Detective Finley stared at the two of them with an eyebrow raised. "Can't deny that either. We have that information and have already started interviewing employees that were there that night. As far as we know though, no one was in Sean's area working the night of the murder." Detective Finley stared at the screen for a moment longer before he cut his eyes over to Naomi. "How do you know all of this? Wait a minute, weren't you involved with a recent case? Your name sounds vaguely familiar."

"I was, and I work for Edmon, but you might have heard my name in connection to Paige Harris and June Liu, who were kidnapped."

"Ah, yes. Although I mostly work homicide, I remember hearing about it."

Naomi nodded her head and gave a tight smile, hoping he wouldn't talk more about the events which had shaken her life forever. As if he'd heard her inner thoughts, Finley stopped.

"Okay, our next move is to keep interviewing people and see if there is any information that Edmon needs to give us related to who was in the building that evening. I'll let you know when I get that information. I'll—" Detective Finley was interrupted by a beep coming from Chief Hughes's desk.

"Chief?"

"Yes?"

You have a meeting with your media advisors before your press conference, and they're waiting for you out here."

"Thank you, Kelly." He turned to his current guests. "I have to go, but I want the three of you to keep me apprised of this investigation. Every discovery you make I want to know about it. The governor is on my back, and we need to show that we are taking steps to find the suspect as soon as possible."

Soon the meeting wrapped up and the couple left the

Henry Daly Building. Naomi and Reed didn't speak until they were both in Reed's black sedan and he had pulled away from the curb.

"Well, that was interesting, to say the least."

Reed didn't say anything as he drove through traffic, having opted to take his car to the Metropolitan Police Department's headquarters versus taking the metro.

"How do you know Detective Finley?"

"We were in the academy together," he said, tapping his fingers on the steering wheel. "We were pretty close but drifted apart after I left the force."

"Interesting. Are you still friends?"

"I guess you could say that," Reed said before flicking on his left turn signal.

"Where are we going? Your condo isn't in this direction."

"I know," he said. "I'm wondering if we might be able to find out more information about Technological Mechanics and their uniform. Wouldn't hurt to stop by their shop."

"That's a good idea," Naomi said.

"I grabbed the address when we were leaving, and it isn't far from the station. In fact, it should be right around here." Reed pointed past Naomi so she, in turn, looked out the passenger side window.

"I would never have guessed these people run a shop that is based in tech services. But I also know you shouldn't judge a book by its cover, or so the old saying goes." The outside of the building looked like it had seen better days. Between the front gate that was in dire need of repair and the sign with Technological Mechanics adorn on it needed to be replaced if the holes in it were any indication.

"Yeah, it looks a little dingy. I'm just hoping the uniform

was legitimate and not someone making a counterfeit product."

Naomi nodded as she waited for Reed to park the car. The two exited the vehicle, and Naomi grabbed Reed's arm before he could walk up to Technological Mechanics.

"You know, I don't know if this would be helpful, but you might be able to ask Levi if he knows anything about this company as well. I mean, I know he's not in the same field, per se, but that doesn't mean they might not have crossed paths." Levi Cannon, a photo analyst, was a college friend of Reed's who sometimes worked with MPD to help them on cases specifically related to photography and clearing up images.

"Good idea. I'll do that once we're done here."

"Let's hope we have something to report after this meeting."

CHAPTER 7

"Sometimes people are more willing to talk when they know the cops are either around or on their way. Sometimes it's the opposite but let's hope this swings in our favor." Reed held the door open so Naomi could step inside.

"A baseball reference? Really?"

"Didn't even realize I said it until I did."

When she crossed over the threshold, a mechanical bell rang, and they made their way to the nearest counter. She assumed before walking into the shop that this would be high-tech and full of life. In comparison to Cyber Sonic, a cybercafé they had visited when looking for Paige, this was a complete one-hundred-and-eighty-degree turn.

The location almost reminded Naomi of a junkyard filled with computer parts. Some of the items Naomi recognized from her own adventures in building her own computers when she was younger. She didn't remember ever having come here for parts, and she knew that she would have remembered it. If the door hadn't been opened, Naomi would have assumed that the place was deserted. Despite the disorganization, Naomi hoped that the owner had some sort of system in order to keep their business running properly.

"Hello."

Naomi turned around, and they were greeted by an older man, as he walked up to the stand behind the counter.

"What can I do for you today?"

"My name is Reed Wright, and this is Naomi." He flashed his private investigator badge at the man. When Naomi looked down at it before Reed put it back in his pocket, it had extra text at the bottom of it, a change since the last time she saw it. It said, 'MPD Investigation,' and she assumed it indicated he was working with the Metropolitan Police Department on a case. "We would like to know if one of your technicians was assigned to Edmon headquarters at 7:30 p.m. on June 28th?"

"That's private information and since I don't see a warrant, I don't think I have to tell you."

Naomi thought he had a good point although she didn't voice her opinion. She was curious to see how Reed would handle that answer.

Reed leaned forward on the counter. "Is it, though? What's your name?"

"Gerald."

"Well, Gerald, you have about ten minutes to tell me everything you know about which one of your technicians was at Edmon headquarters." Reed paused to swipe through his phone and pulled up a screenshot of surveillance footage. The image was of the person wearing the uniform entering through the front doors.

"The police are on their way," Naomi chimed in. "They're

headed here because this is a part of an investigation, and the person wearing this uniform is a suspect in a murder."

Gerald's eyes widened and darted between Naomi and Reed, as if he couldn't believe what they just said. "Uh, let me pull up my records. I don't want any trouble with the police."

"Didn't think so," Naomi said as she folded her arms.

Reed tapped his index finger on the counter. "Yeah, I kind of figured that this would be the case."

"Usually, if someone on my staff is called to the Edmon, they go sometime during the day. Edmon has rules about that."

Reed glanced at Naomi before back to Gerald. "We have a problem here, then, because this person was wearing one of your uniforms in the evening after the work day was over."

"I know, and if it was one of my people, it was during their off hours or someone else bought or stole one of our uniforms." Gerald turned to his computer. "Simon. Open attendance logs."

He didn't say anything for a while as he scanned the document before him. Naomi watched his facial reactions to see if it would give it away. He then looked at the image on Reed's phone before once again, turning his attention back to his computer monitor. It took a couple of moments, but she saw him jerk his head back quickly in shock.

"What do you find?"

"That's strange. It seems as if it was Dwayne Clarence, one of my technicians, who has been out for a couple of days. We thought he was sick."

"What do you mean 'thought'?"

Gerald didn't answer Naomi's question, but continued to reread the screen in front of him, flabbergasted. "But he's the only person here. Unless someone just didn't clock out, he's the only outlier here on the schedule."

"Has he been out to do any work at Edmon recently?" Naomi asked.

Gerald performed a search in the scheduling application. "Yes, but it was a few months ago."

"Has anyone heard from him since the last time he was at work?" Reed grabbed his phone, giving his full attention to the older man.

Gerald looked through his notes before he shook his head. "Not that I'm aware. He should have come to the office today, and he didn't."

Naomi and Reed shared a look again. "Can we have Dwayne's address? MPD will do a wellness check on him."

"Sure, here it is."

Gerald turned the computer screen, and Reed held up his phone to scan Dwayne's address. The directions to Dwayne's place immediately popped up as an option. "MPD will still be here in approximately seven minutes. Do you have any follow up questions for me?"

Gerald shook his head, growing pale underneath the artificial lighting. "I'm happy to work with MPD. Don't want any trouble with the police."

Naomi almost felt sorry for the older man. She said, "We understand. Thank you for your help." The couple exited the shop and walked back to Reed's car.

Reed handed his phone to Naomi. "I need you to send a message to Finley about everything that just occurred at Technological Mechanics and tell him we are on our way to Dwayne's home."

"Yeah, I can do that no problem."

Reed pulled out of the parking spot while Naomi sent a message to Detective Finley from Reed's phone. Once she was done, Reed reached over and called someone from his dashboard. When their face popped up on the screen, Naomi couldn't help but smile.

"Reed! Naomi! How are you doing?"

Naomi smiled at the enthusiastic voice blaring through the speaker phone. It had been a while since she'd heard Levi's boisterous voice. She could see that Levi was sitting in his office based on what she remembered from the last time she was there.

"I'm good. We are on our way to talk with someone about a case."

"Wait, you're both on your way to interview someone?" Surprise passed over Levi's face, along with mild amusement.

Reed shook his head. "Long story. Hi, Levi!"

"What can I do for two of my favorite people?"

"Do you know anything about Technological Mechanics?" Reed navigated the car through traffic.

Levi tilted his head. "I haven't heard anything bad about them. They do good work. I've gone in to have a couple of machines fixed over the years and have had no issues."

"Nothing weird about their operations?"

"They tend to be old school when it comes to a lot of things, but I don't think there is anything wrong with that. I didn't get any bad vibes from them and recommended several friends and associates who were having issues to them."

Reed nodded. "Listen, thanks for the feedback on them. We are on our way to talk to someone else, but I'll talk to you soon. We should hang out when our schedules free up."

"Sounds like a plan. Talk to you both later." He gave a quick salute.

"Bye!" Naomi said just before Levi's face disappeared from the screen.

It didn't take long for Naomi and Reed to arrive at Dwayne's house since he didn't live far away from his job. Reed parked in front of his apartment building. He reached toward his dashboard and clicked a few buttons before the dashboard opened up and Reed pulled out a pistol.

Naomi did a double take. "I assumed you owned a gun, but this is the first time I'm seeing it."

"I own a few. I have this one in this special case here in case of emergencies."

"Is this an emergency?"

Reed glanced at her. "If this guy is tied to a murder, it is." As he was opening up his door, another car sped to a stop in front of them. He opened the driver's side window.

"Finley. That was fast."

"Perks of having sirens on top of this vehicle," he said. "I've got this from here."

"Funny. We're going in there together. This badge says I'm allowed to do that."

Detective Finley sighed. Naomi still couldn't pinpoint whether he was grateful or annoyed to have to be working the case with them. "Fine, come on."

The couple waited for Detective Finley to park his car, and soon, they were on their way up the stairs to reach Dwayne's apartment. Detective Finley turned to look over his shoulder at the couple briefly. "By the way, we've confirmed that Edmon's security was breached on the night of the murder, hence how our suspect was able to get into the building."

When they reached it, the detective put his arm up, stopping Naomi and Reed from proceeding.

"We don't know what we are walking into," Detective Finley said as he looked down at the gun in his hand. "You still know how to use one?"

"You're hilarious." Reed checked the gun before he pulled Naomi behind him, shielding her with his body as a precaution.

Detective Finley knocked on the door, but no one responded.

Naomi looked at Reed, who had a look of pure concentration on his face. She took a small step back as several red flags raised in her mind. Who didn't tell their job that they needed to take another day off, if you were scheduled to return to work?

Detective Finley knocked again. "Dwayne. Dwayne Clarence. This is the police. Open up."

"Are you looking for Dwayne?"

The group turned to find an older woman standing at a door across the hall. "Yes, we are," Detective Finley answered. "Have you seen him?"

"It's been a few days," she said. "Is he in trouble?"

"That we don't know for sure, ma'am," Detective Finley responded. "But why don't you get back inside, just in case?"

"Okay," she said and slowly closed the door behind her.

"Are we going to need a warrant to get into his apartment?"

Detective Finley glanced at Reed after his question but didn't say anything. He knocked on the door again, this time a little bit harder. "You're my back up, Reed."

He made a move to try to break down the door but

stopped. When Naomi looked more closely, it was clear the door opened a smidge.

"Someone reinforced the door with some type of adhesive, which raises a lot of questions. It also tells me someone couldn't lock the door." Detective Finley drew his weapon and walked inside first. "I'm going to make sure the place is clear, and then you guys can come in, if there's nothing here."

"I can come in with you. You know, as back up." Reed smirked, throwing Detective Finley's line back at him.

The detective's shoulders relaxed a bit, dry humor coming out. "Just like old times."

Reed shook his head and turned to Naomi. "You stay out here, and once we know everything is safe, you can come in."

Naomi nodded just before Reed squeezed her hand and entered the apartment, closing the door slightly behind him, mostly blocking her view. Keeping a good distance between her and the door, Naomi waited for the go-ahead to enter the location. Minutes felt like an eternity before Reed came back to the front door with a grim look on his face.

"What happened?"

With the door opened again, Naomi could see the chaos inside Dwayne's apartment. Things were everywhere, a table was askew, papers were strewn about the room. Her eyes danced over to a lit room that she could see Detective Finley standing in. Based on the positioning and the shower curtain in the background of the mirror, she could assume it was Dwayne's bathroom. Reed's voice cut through the thoughts flying around her head.

"You might want to sit out in the car, because it looks as if Dwayne is dead in his bathroom. Door was reinforced with the same adhesive as on the front door to keep any signs of his death enclosed in that space, but now it's only a matter of time before the smell of the body is everywhere."

That was when Naomi got her first whiff of the stench. "Yeah, I'm going to take you up on that offer. I'll see you soon."

"Actually, why don't you take my car back to the condo? I might be here for a little while, try and clear this out." Reed grimaced as the smell started to hit him as well.

Naomi nodded. "Okay, sounds like a plan." She thought about making a joke about him freely allowing her to drive his baby, but she refrained, because it was neither the time nor place. Reed handed over his keys.

"Oh, one more thing."

"Yeah?"

"Make sure you check to see if he has his uniform."

Reed's face was grim. "It's the first thing on my list. See you back at the condo."

Naomi quickly hurried back down the hall, but something in her gut told her it wouldn't be there.

CHAPTER 8

Naomi walked into Reed's condo and tossed his keys on the counter. She toed off her shoes, heading into the living room. She knew she'd missed Chief Hughes' press conference, but given the twenty-four-hour news cycle, she wouldn't be surprised if she was able to catch some clips of it.

She sat back on the couch and turned on the television. After flicking through a couple of channels before settling on the one she wanted, it only took a couple of minutes before the station started playing clips from the press conference.

Chief Hughes was the perfect example of strength and calmness during a tense and stressful situation. He explained the facts of the case, and Naomi noticed he didn't mention Dwayne Clarence at all so she wondered if Detective Finley had told him yet or not. To her, that made sense because there wasn't a direct link between Dwayne's murder and Sean's even though she thought they were on a path that would lead to both of them being connected.

Reporters asked questions, and one reporter's questions

stood out in particular to Naomi. "Chief Hughes, it seems as if Edmon is having a tough year, wouldn't you say? Do you see this as being the work of someone acting alone, or is it someone you believe to be working with a group? Should the residents of D.C. be concerned about public safety?"

Chief Hughes took a moment before he responded. "I won't speak on behalf of Edmon because I'm not in charge over there. I've heard that Mr. Billings will be hosting his own press conference at a later time so you can ask him then. I know, in the past, we have asked the public to remain on high alert. As of now, however, there is no indication that there is a need for the public to be alarmed. As always, we encourage people to be vigilant, and MPD is doing everything we can to bring this murderer down so justice will be served. Thank you so much and have a good rest of your day."

Naomi turned the television off and walked into the kitchen to get a glass of water. When she returned to the living room, she found herself pacing back and forth, waiting on word from Reed. She hoped either he'd walk through the door or he'd send her a message. When neither happened, she knew she needed to do something to both keep her occupied and to push the investigation further along. That's when a memory was triggered in her mind, and she raced to her laptop.

When June was kidnapped by Naomi's half-brother, Naomi had been able to tap into security footage from Edmon through her laptop. She wondered if that feature was still available or if they had completely switched everything over to the new security system. A few clicks led her to the answer. It seemed they were still in the process of migrating everything over, including the camera angle that had helped catch

Jett Washington leading June away from the Edmon offices a few months prior, but not all of the cameras inside the building had been switched over yet. If this helped to solve this case, she would jump for joy. The problem now became whether or not the camera that would show the suspect had been switched over. If it had, she was out of luck, but if it hadn't, there might be a chance she could see the suspect's face. Naomi spent the next twenty minutes scouring the various cameras, trying to find just a small glimpse of a suspect, but nothing popped.

"This asshole isn't a ghost," she mumbled to herself. There was more to this that she just hadn't found yet.

She flipped back through and found footage from the eighth floor. Only one camera was shining on a bank of elevators. Naomi found the timestamp she was looking for, around 7:35 p.m., and watched for any movement. She didn't want to fast forward in case she missed something.

After staring at the video for several minutes, she gasped. A figure dressed in dark clothes exited the elevator and walked toward where Naomi knew Sean's cubicle was located.

"That must be the person who killed Sean."

The next thing she noticed was when the person exited the elevator, they weren't wearing the Technological Mechanics uniform. *Where did you stash it?* Naomi prayed the person would turn to look at the camera, but they didn't. She paused the footage and tried again to uncover anything else from the eighth floor but couldn't find anything. Her only hope was this person would show back up in front of this camera, but time continued to fly by, and there was no sight of the mysterious person.

"Come on…. Come on…. Come back the way you came."

She waited, jiggling her leg anxiously. It didn't take her long to realize that the person didn't come back toward the elevators. They must have left through a separate exit. That shouldn't have surprised her given that the staircases in Edmon were open in case of a fire or another emergency and were only locked on the outside, making it easier to exit and almost impossible to enter from there. It also further confirmed that the person knew the layout of Edmon's building well.

When Reed entered his condo, he broke Naomi's concentration on the video in front of her. He closed the door and walked toward her just as she asked, "How'd everything go?"

Before he answered, Reed sat down on his couch and closed his eyes. Naomi gave him a moment of silence and waited patiently for him to speak.

"About as well as it could have been. I keep comparing Sean Barlow's murder scene to the one I just saw and I'm not sure which I would say was worse."

"I'm so sorry." Naomi could see the stress in his face and the tension in his muscles.

He opened his eyes and gave her a half smile. "It's not your fault, but it seems as if we have another senseless, tragic tragedy with two families that will probably never be whole again."

"Do you think he walked in on the theft and that's why he's dead? Poor guy, died for something as ridiculous as a work uniform, that's so messed up."

"Potentially, but we'd have to find out more information to be able to declare that. If that is the case, he was in the wrong place at the wrong time." Reed rubbed the back of his neck.

Naomi cleared her throat. "Speaking of more information, did you find anything that would help us with the Sean Barlow case?"

"Not much, unfortunately. So far, other than both of them being involved with tech in some capacity and Dwayne's uniform ending up at Edmon, these two have no connection to each other. Not related, no mutual friends, didn't frequent the same places, etcetera."

"I might have found his uniform. Kind of."

Reed's eyebrows raised. "What do you mean you might have found his uniform? You've been here the whole time, right?"

Naomi side-eyed him, wondering where he was going with this. "Yes, and I didn't scratch your precious baby on the way back to your condo."

"I didn't think you did. I trust your driving."

Naomi's expression relaxed. "That's a new development. Anyway, do you remember when we were looking at surveillance video for June a few months back, and we discovered Edmon hadn't transferred all of their video feed over to their new server?"

She could see Reed was trying to follow where she was going. "Don't tell me they still haven't switched everything over. It's been months."

"I know, and they transferred more of the video feeds over to the protective server they are planning on using, but not all. There was one camera on the eighth floor that showed someone leaving the elevator, within an hour of Sean's murder. And they weren't in the uniform."

"So, what you're saying is if we saw the murderer on the

eighth-floor camera, there is a good chance that the uniform is more than likely still in the Edmon building."

Naomi nodded her head. "If I had to bet money, I would guess it is still at Edmon."

"Fascinating. I'll have to check in with Finley about this, but I don't believe Edmon shared this footage with MPD."

Naomi did a double take. "Seriously?" What was the point of them holding this footage back?

"Could have been an oversight, or maybe the information wasn't relayed to me. In any case, I'll talk to Finley about it. After that, you and I are going to take a break."

"We are?"

"Yes, because while we are investigating a murder, having time to ourselves is also important. And chances are, we aren't going to find out anything else tonight. So why don't we spend it by doing something enjoyable together."

Naomi leaned back with a small smile on her face. "I like the way you think, Mr. Wright."

"Sometimes, I have good ideas."

Naomi snorted before Reed continued.

"Is there anything in particular that you want to do?"

"Honestly, I could do just about anything, and it's only seven o'clock. There are plenty of restaurants still open if you just wanted to grab a quick bite to eat. Nothing too fancy because I don't want to try to figure out something to wear. I am perfectly comfortable in these jeans."

"We can walk around for a bit before we pick a place to eat and watch the sunset."

"I like this idea. How long will it take you to get ready?"

Naomi looked at her outfit. "I'll probably just fix my hair and put on some lip balm, so less than ten minutes."

"All right, I'll see you in ten minutes." Reed paused and then said, "Actually, I should probably wash off the grime from today, so I'm going to take a quick shower. Let's make that fifteen minutes."

"Okay. Let me just grab some of my things out of the bathroom, and then it's all yours."

The couple stood up and walked toward the bathroom. Reed softly grabbed her hand and pulled her toward the main bedroom, which was connected to the bathroom.

"You know, we could just stay in and do another fun activity instead."

Naomi gave up fighting the smile that appeared on her face. She chuckled slightly before she said, "We can take a raincheck on that and save it for when we get back. I'm dying to spend some time with you...outside."

"I'm holding you to that." He gave her a dazzling smile and walked into the bathroom. Naomi followed him and quickly grabbed her things and headed to the guest bathroom. She left her curly hair resting on her shoulders, only taking the opportunity to fluff it out, but made sure to have a hair tie on her wrist, in case it was still humid, and she needed to throw her hair up quickly.

After applying the lip balm, Naomi made a last-minute decision to change her shirt. She was pretty sure she had a navy t-shirt here at Reed's house and thought she could toss it on before leaving.

She walked back into Reed's room, just as he strolled out of the bathroom, towel drying his hair as he went. Naomi walked over to one of the dresser drawers he had designated for her and soon all doubt was removed when she found the shirt she was looking for. She quickly unbuttoned and removed the shirt she had been wearing all day, and as she was putting the t-shirt on, Reed chimed in.

"Have you changed your mind about going out?"

Naomi looked over her shoulder at him. "No, we deserve to go out like normal people do." She finished pulling the shirt down over her abdomen.

"I'm just kidding."

"But are you?" She raised an eyebrow.

"It might be a little bit of both," he said.

Naomi shook her head. "Are you ready?"

"Almost. Give me a minute."

True to his word, he was soon ready to go, and together, the couple set off to enjoy a romantic night on the town.

CHAPTER 9

The couple took their time walking back to Reed's condo as they enjoyed the quick date that they had thrown together last minute.

"Do you want to stop somewhere and get dessert?"

Naomi glanced at him out of the corner of her eye. "Is this your way of saying you want to have sex when we get home?"

The tip of Reed's tongue ran across his lips before he chuckled. "No, I was thinking of ice cream, but if that's what you want to do..."

Naomi felt her cheeks grow hot. "I'm never one to turn down ice cream."

"A new creamery opened up a couple of blocks away. Let's head there and try it out."

They walked over to the creamery and Naomi got cookie dough ice cream while Reed got mint chocolate chip. They both polished off their ice cream cones while taking a leisurely walk in Reed's neighborhood as they admired Washington, D.C. at night.

"Dinner and a movie is a classic, yet, one of the best date

night activities," Naomi said as she wiped her mouth with a napkin.

"That it is," Reed said as he let Naomi into his condo before following behind her.

"We need to take the time to do that more often."

That was true, especially recently. A lot of their dates ended up being at home, with one of them cooking dinner while the other was finishing up work. If Naomi had to be honest, it was usually she who was finishing work while Reed was cooking. She was annoyed about it, and she had a feeling that he was, too, until he admitted it.

"There's one thing that has been on my mind this entire time, though."

Reed's words took her out of the thoughts about them having to take out more time for one another. His voice took on a deeper tone, warming her soul as his words danced over her body. But what fun would this be if she didn't tease him a bit? "And what's that?"

"You and my raincheck, of course."

He was already standing near her, so it took him no time until he had her face in his hands. His gunmetal blue eyes stared into her chocolate brown ones before they migrated to her lips. He studied them lightly before he leant down to kiss her. All of the stress from the case they were working on together came out in their kiss, as they were determined to leave thoughts of the case behind just for the night. Their tongues tangled up with one another, swirling around as they performed intricate movements that only they knew. His hands moved over her face, down her body, starting a fire within her that was bursting to come out.

He moved his head down her throat where he alternated

between leaving soft kisses and nibbles on his way down. Naomi's moans intensified the further he moved down, begging him with her noises to continue having his way with her. Reed wasn't one to deny her and continued touching her everywhere, stirring her into a frenzy. Out of nowhere, Reed lifted her up and she wrapped her legs around his waist. She didn't care where he was taking her, as long as they were together.

He held her around the waist with one arm while the other one swiped away all of the junk mail and papers he had on his dining room table. It was obvious that he had the same feelings as her, desperate to touch and get as close to her as physically possible. Nothing was going to stand in the way of that.

Once she was seated on the table, Reed focused on her breasts. He quickly removed her shirt and she snatched off her bra which proved to be a hindrance to his overall goal.

"You do realize we eat here sometimes, right?"

Reed stopped what he was doing and looked at her. "And it will be thoroughly cleaned when we're done. But you'll never forget the moment that we made love, right here on this table."

He was quickly back to work, his lips moved feverishly from one nipple to the other, as if trying to find salvation from the trauma they'd both witnessed. Naomi's whimpers grew louder and louder due to Reed's teasing tongue and teeth until he slowed down a bit. He kissed down her body and landed just above the waist band to her jeans. He left a couple of kisses before he pulled back and his fingers took over, unbuttoning her jeans and sliding both her jeans and panties down her legs. He caressed her thighs with his hands and lips before he made his way between her thighs.

"It's funny how I'm basically naked and you're still fully clothed. I swear this is a common occurrence between us," Naomi let out breathlessly.

"It's because I'm usually too focused on removing your clothes, that I forget about my own."

"That won't do. I want to feel your skin on mine."

"Easy fix." Reed got rid of his clothes in record time, not even giving Naomi a moment to stare down his perfect physique before he was back on her.

He made his way back to her core, where his ministrations continued, causing her to moan and groan under his touch. Before long, he stood up and pulled her legs toward him, lining himself up with her body. Inch by inch, he entered her, driving her wild the more he moved. She thanked every day when they decided to forgo condoms and use other methods of protection. When he couldn't move anymore, he leaned down and laid a luscious kiss on her mouth, leaving her begging for more.

"Reed, are you—"

Her words were cut off because he moved, quickly finding a rhythm that made Naomi close her eyes and arch her back in pleasure. When she looked back at him, all she could see was hunger in his eyes and she was willing to bet that her eyes reflected the same. His hands on her waist helped guide them both as his pace picked up and the musical notes that their groans made played overhead.

When they both crossed over into paradise together, the moment was magical with nothing that could be heard outside of their heavy breathing as they recovered from the love making they just took part in.

Reed didn't move to get off of her and she didn't want him

to. Having his skin touching hers was her nirvana even if in the back in her mind she knew they would have to move soon.

"You know, you're right. I'll never look at this table the same again."

"It truly feels wonderful being out in the fresh morning air," Naomi said as she pumped her arms by her sides. "Not jogging over the last few days has left me in a bit of a funk."

"Trust me, I could tell."

Naomi glared at her boyfriend but didn't stop moving. The fresh air entered her body, and as she exhaled, it helped propel her down the block they were running down. The light breeze through her curls was all she could have hoped for as her feet hit the sidewalk in a satisfying rhythm. Her half marathon training had been on pause since her life had been in a tailspin and she knew that at some point in the future, she'd get back to it. As of now, running for enjoyment and cardio were her main focuses. "Working out is great for getting the brain moving and thoughts flowing. For example, I want to talk to Sean's boss today, if we can."

Reed looked at her curiously. "Why is that?"

The two came to a halt at a stop light, and Naomi took the opportunity to stretch while Reed jogged in place. "Because I want to know exactly what Sean was working on. Since he was murdered at work, I wonder if it had something to do with a project he was working on."

"That's a good idea. I'm sure MPD is investigating it too, but you would have more knowledge on the subject matter."

When the light turned green, Naomi and Reed started jogging again.

Reed glanced at Naomi. "There's only one way to find out. We need to make some phone calls."

"Barry Stein, who is Sean's boss, shouldn't be hard to track down. I will say I do know more about him than I did Sean." That fact still somewhat bothered Naomi.

"Let's finish up this jog and make a plan for how to tackle this."

The couple finished up their run and as they were walking through the front door of Reed's condo, his cell phone rang. Naomi popped into the kitchen for two bottles of water, passing one to him. Reed smiled his thanks and Reed listened for several seconds before he said, "Hey, hold on, I'm going to put you on speaker so Naomi can hear you." He pulled the phone away from his ear and tapped the screen. "Okay, you're good."

Finley's voice came through the speaker. "Hey, I wanted to tell you that you guys picked up on a great lead. The footage from the night of the murder helped us find the uniform that belonged to Dwayne Clarence and Technological Mechanics."

"That's great." Naomi's mouth was slightly ajar.

"Based on an assumption, we think the suspect hoped the uniform would end up in a garbage truck headed to who knows where, but instead someone must have found it, and turned it in to Edmon security. We're running tests on it now, but we're not sure if we'll find any DNA to tie it to a person."

Reed took a gulp of water and cleared his throat. "That officially links the two murders together."

"It does," Finley answered. "Also makes us wonder if this is one person acting alone, or if there are more people involved in whatever scheme it is. This is not to say that this couldn't be one person acting solo, but we are definitely keeping our options open that it might be at least two, if not more."

Reed ran his hand down Naomi's back, providing some comfort to her as if he knew that tidbit of news freaked her out, before turning back to the speaker phone. "Thanks for the update, Finley. We're going to go and talk to Sean's boss to see if we can glean any more information that he might have."

"MPD already talked to Barry Stein."

"I know, but you also didn't have the best database expert who could speak his language."

Naomi smiled at his compliment as Detective Finley continued, "That would have been helpful. I'll send the transcripts over so you can take a look at them."

"That'd be helpful. That way we aren't doubling back over something that's already been covered."

"Exactly," Finley replied. "Well, if you guys need anything else, please let me know, and we'll do the same."

"Okay. Talk to you soon."

"Bye."

Naomi stretched, finally taking a drink to cool her parched throat. "I'm going to shower while we wait for Finley to get the interview to us."

"Do you want some company? Saving the water and all that?"

Naomi could feel her cheeks growing warm. "No, because we'll spend way too much time in the shower, therefore wasting water."

* * *

"Did you get the transcripts?" Naomi asked as she stepped out of the bathroom and went over to her bag to pull out the clothing she'd brought to wear for the day. She quickly dressed, feeling Reed's eyes on her as she did so.

"I did." Reed smirked as he watched her. "Come on, I'll show you."

He pulled her to him and kissed her before leading her back out to the living room where he'd set his laptop on the coffee table. They sat down on the sofa, and he pulled up the interview and the transcript. Naomi and Reed took their time watching the video, comparing it to the transcript, and didn't find any discrepancies.

"It barely goes into detail about what Sean was working on, which could be a reason why he was killed. Only speaking about that from experience with being blackmailed by my father. Granted, I didn't die."

Reed glanced at her when she said, 'die.' She could feel the coolness from his eyes, and it was clear he didn't appreciate her comment. "Don't say that."

"But it's the truth. I wonder how quickly we can get in to see Barry," Naomi muttered. She looked up from the computer. "Did MPD get a warrant for Sean's work computer?"

"Finley hasn't mentioned it, but I would assume so. I'll follow up."

"If not, it might be wise to get a clearance for MPD to get access to his laptop and see if anything is amiss. Only potential issue is that the laptop is Edmon property, and I'm sure there is quite a lot of red tape that will need to be cut to really get it," Naomi said as she sat back on her heels. It might be a pain in the ass, but the reward could be worth it. But Edmon was under no obligation to hand it over, unless there was a court order in place, and there might be some hesitation because their cloud server was involved.

"Let me contact Barry and see if we can set up a meeting for today." Naomi pulled out her phone and messaged Barry Stein on Edmon's messenger system.

Naomi: Hey, Barry, I know that we don't know each other well, but I was wondering if I could talk to you about everything going on surrounding the circumstances with Sean's death.

Barry: Is it urgent? I'm still reeling from losing not only a colleague, but someone I considered a friend.

"I feel bad about pressing him on this," she said.

Reed came over and looked at the messages. "But he might have some valuable information that might lead us to find out why Sean was killed."

Naomi swallowed the doubt in her mind before she typed the next message.

Naomi: I'm working with MPD to try to find out why this happened to Sean and who did it. I think you might be able to clue us in on a few things. And it would be great if we could talk to you sometime soon. The sooner, the better if you want to find out what happened to him as soon as possible.

Barry: I already talked to MPD.

Naomi: I know, but I have some questions I would like to ask that I think only you'd be able to answer. I apologize for being so pushy on this, but I want to find out who could have possibly done this.

    Barry: *I want that too. How about you come over to my place?*
    Naomi: *That'd be great. When?*
    Barry: *How about in an hour?*
    Naomi: *Sounds good. Send me your address. I will be there soon.*

* * *

"WE NEED to head out to meet Barry in five."

"I'll be right there." Naomi turned off the faucet and watched as the droplets of water dripped from her hand. She turned around to grab a towel and chuckled because she assumed it was another one of the features Reed's sister had recommended while she decorated his place.

As she was drying her hands, her eyes shifted to watch herself in the mirror. Her golden-brown skin looked slightly dull, and Naomi could attribute that to stress. She wondered what she had gotten herself into as her heart rate picked up. Two people had been murdered in the span of a couple of days, and it felt as if they weren't any closer to figuring out who had done it. Naomi could feel the strain of the stressful situation weighing her down as she thought about what was at stake. She took a moment to do some deep breathing exercises as she tried to release the tension in her body. Her nerves were buzzing about this meeting with Barry as she hoped it would lead to a solid path they could travel down, getting them closer to whoever did this. If this wasn't their big break, she didn't know where they would go from there, outside of potentially waiting for MPD to find something for them to track down.

Naomi came out of the bathroom and gave Reed a tight smile. "I'm ready."

"Good. Let's go."

The ride to Barry's was mostly silent, and Naomi attributed that to being stuck in her own thoughts about everything going on. When they arrived at Barry's home, they were a couple minutes early.

"Are you ready to do this?"

Reed stopped Naomi with his question, and she paused before opening the black sedan's passenger side door. She wondered if he was picking up on her nervous energy. "I am."

Reed walked up the steps first and identified himself at the door before Naomi did the same, showing Reed had come with her. When the door opened, the couple were greeted by a middle-aged woman with a polite smile. "Are you guys here to talk to Barry? He mentioned someone would be stopping by for a meeting today."

"Yes, we are." Naomi stepped forward and smiled.

"I'm Barry's wife, Regina, and I'll show you to his office. He had a couple of emails he needed to finish sending or he would have answered the door."

"Thank you so much," Naomi said, and Regina closed the door before stepping around them to lead her guests down the long hallway.

"I hope you had no trouble finding the house or parking. Sometimes it can be hit or miss," she said, making small conversation as she led them toward Barry's office.

"No, we had no trouble. Parked a couple houses down. Looks like we got lucky," Reed said.

"That's good. If you need anything, please let me know.

Here we are." She gestured to the office door, knocking. "Barry, Naomi and Reed are here to see you."

A couple seconds later, the door swung open, and Barry looked at his wife, Reed and Naomi. "Thanks, honey," he said as he leaned down to give her a quick kiss. He then turned to the other couple. "Come on. Let's get this over with."

He gestured for Naomi and Reed to enter his office and sit down at a smaller table. "Oh, I should have asked if you guys want anything. Can I get you water? I'm sure we might have some cookies available, but I'm not one hundred percent positive about that."

"I'm okay, thanks," Naomi said, and Reed followed with a similar response. "Well, we didn't want to take up much of your time, because I know you're grieving, and we know you already talked to MPD. We wanted to follow up with a few questions of our own related to what project Sean was working on."

"Ah, yes. Sean was working on a cloud server project."

That got her attention. "Which cloud server project?"

Barry's eyes wandered around the room. "It was supposed to be top secret. I was only made vaguely aware of the server because I'm Sean's manager."

Wait. Did Edmon have more than one top secret server but could it be the same one I'm working on?

"Is this the server that Cyber Edge exists on?"

"I could only assume. It was the first time I've heard of this secret server existing and there've been rumors about Edmon having the file for years so it wouldn't surprise me if it was there.

Visions of her father threatening her to get the data out of that file and into a database or else he would harm Paige flew through her mind. Cyber Edge was a file that contained vital information about many high-profile people around the world. As far as she knew, she'd been the only one who was granted access to it in recent months by Edmon's system administrator. So why would Sean be on this server as well?

"That's the same thing I'm working on and have been working on for Edmon for a while."

Barry tilted his head. "That can't be. The only developer who was working on that project was Sean. He was specifically picked for that project."

What Barry said triggered another thought in Naomi's mind: She and Sean never worked together. It would make sense for them to collaborate if it meant working toward the same goal. So why hadn't she and Sean, or hell, Barry and Doug been told?

"I swear, I've been working on it, and I have been trying to figure out why no one seemed to know."

"Doug's your manager, right?"

Naomi nodded. "And I'll have to confirm with him, but I don't think he knew Sean was working on the server either."

"And if we knew you were also working on this project, it would have made sense for at least you two to meet or to have a meeting with all four of us to make sure no work was being duplicated."

"And I want to know why. Are there other developers working on this project? I have no idea. As far as I know, no one on my team works on this, besides me."

"Sean was the only one working on this project from my team. I was told to make sure Sean was on it, because he was one of the best of the best."

"Who told you to put him on that project, if you can share?"

"Came from the big boss."

Naomi's eyes widened. "And he told you to make sure Sean was available for this project?"

"Yep, never happened before in my twenty years at Edmon." Barry mindlessly played with a pen while Naomi sat there, shocked. "Usually, I'm able to give my team projects to do depending on what lands on my desk and I'm sure Doug does the same for you, but the message to have Sean on that project came from the top down."

She wondered if something similar had happened in her case too. She'd thought she had been working her hardest to be available for a high-profile position and she was happy to be assigned the cloud server, but what if it was just handed to her without it being a result of her merit? Was this connected to all of the events that had occurred with Morris last year?

She set those thoughts aside and said, "So what was it about Sean that made him ideal for this project?"

"He was the best on my team. Not sure how I'm going to replace him."

"Who knew he would be there that night? I mean, did he often work late like that? Why didn't he take it home to work remote? Was there something he was doing specifically that he needed to be at Edmon to do it?" Naomi knew that certain aspects of the server could only be accessed on sight due to security protocols so she wondered if he might have been working on that there.

"I did, maybe a few others from the team because he mentioned it in a work group chat." Barry nodded and then shrugged. "I guess he did, the secret server project as you know is a priority, so if he was making a breakthrough, he would have kept at it until he was finished with that section. Sean was pretty dedicated. As for whether or not he could have done it from home, I don't know. I'd have to look into that."

"Can I take a look at what he was doing for the project? Maybe he was on a track that I wasn't, and I can incorporate his ideas into mine, and this could be a legacy for him," she suggested.

"I'll have to check in with Wilson since he was the person he was reporting to about it."

"Okay, well, if there is anything else you can think of, let me know." She stood up.

"I will."

"Thanks again for speaking with us," Reed added as they headed to the door.

The group exchanged pleasantries, and Barry showed Naomi and Reed to the door. Once he'd closed the door, Reed said, "That was a bombshell of a conversation."

Naomi walked down Barry's porch steps before she whispered, "Yeah, it was."

Her mood change caused Reed to look at her. "What's wrong?"

"As I was wrapping up the conversation just now, I started second-guessing a lot of my achievements at Edmon. If Barry was told to put Sean on this specific server project, I wonder if Doug was also told the same thing about me. I don't know how I feel about that."

"It could also be that you both were phenomenal in your field and were doing great work at Edmon, that they knew they could trust you to be on this project."

"That's what I would love to be the case but having the CEO request it is not how Edmon does things. Someone as high up as Wilson wouldn't, usually didn't get into the weeds on things like this. Managers would know if the subordinates could handle a project such as this. I find it odd." It made her wonder if there were bigger things at play here. A whining noise flew past Naomi's ear, causing her to jump back slightly.

"What the heck was that?" she asked.

"What?"

"You didn't hear that?"

Reed shook his head, and Naomi bent down and picked something up.

"Do you know what this is?" she asked as she handed over what she found on the ground. Reed briefly examined it, and Naomi watched as his eyes became narrower, anger forming in them. He looked around before he grabbed her arm. "Stay close to the ground and move quickly. We need to get into the car right now."

CHAPTER 11

"*R*eed, what was that?"

Instead of answering her, Reed locked the doors of his vehicle and started the engine. "Someone tried to either knock one of us out or kill us, depending on whatever substance is in that vial you have there." He pulled out of the parking spot and sped down the street.

"What?" Naomi exclaimed. She stared at the tube that Reed laid on the center console before looking back up. "You can't be serious. This looks like something that would come out of a high-tech dart guns."

"Exactly. That's what it is, and someone was more than likely aiming at you, but it missed. Barely."

Naomi picked the tube up and examined it. Although the material looked and felt like glass, there was no way it was because the dart would have burst on impact. Nondescript clear liquid sloshed back in forth inside it. Naomi put the tube back down on the console, not wanting to accidentally spill whatever was inside.

"I've never seen anything like it."

"I have. It's a bit hard to get, but not impossible. Don't know if it's traceable, however."

Fury vibrated off of him as he drove through D.C. The silence that passed between the two of them did nothing to stave his anger.

"You know what? I wonder if the shot was just a warning. The person who shot this was so close to hitting you, to the point where you heard it fly past you, and they missed. Not only that, as far as we know, they didn't try to shoot another one." He wiped his mouth, and she could see him slightly shaking. "I want to know who tried to hurt you, and if it's the last thing I do, I'm going to kill them."

His words sent a chill down Naomi's spine, and she knew he meant it. The muscles in his jaw rippled and his hands clenched the steering wheel as he tried to focus on navigating the car so that he could get them back to his condo safely. The only thing on his mind was finding out who did this.

Naomi laid a hand on his thigh. "I'm fine, everyone is fine. We need to turn this in to the police, because I assume you don't have a lab hiding somewhere at your place."

That made Reed smirk, helping to ease some of the tension in the car. Naomi was happy to put a small smile back on his face for however long it would stay there.

"We also need to find out if Barry has any sort of surveillance set up on his house and if we can see if there were any people or cars near his house just before we showed up. Unless whoever shot that dart has been watching Barry, they didn't have much time to set up and get away."

"Okay, I'm going to call Barry while we head back to the condo. I can't see someone like him not having some sort of cameras in and around his house. Hopefully, we'll have something to check out as we're walking through the door."

* * *

NAOMI AND REED found themselves at the dining room table doing nothing close to what they had done the last time they sat at this table. They were staring at an image of a car with a partial license plate.

"That's a damn good picture of that car. Don't have to call Levi to fix this one up," Reed said as he sat back in the chair.

"I agree. Can you or Detective Finley run this against a database to see if we can figure out who the owner is?"

Barry did have security cameras outside of his home, and luckily, the range extended to the street. His camera had caught images of a car racing down the street after Reed and Naomi had driven off, but the couple hadn't noticed it on the way back to Reed's condo so they assumed that the driver hadn't followed them. There was a small chance the car was related to the incident in front of Barry's house. Since his street was busy and rarely had parking spots, there was a chance this car was looking for parking, too, and wasn't related to the attack on Naomi, but it wouldn't hurt to run the data they had.

Naomi spoke up again. "Let's call in all the possibilities of what the last number of that license plate might be to Detective Finley and see if he can pick up on anything. Plus, maybe he'll be able to tell us what was in that dart. I'm glad the lab was able to come by and pick the vial up."

"Sounds good to me. I'm going to head into my office to take a look at what we have evidence wise on this case."

"I'll come with."

The two walked into Reed's office. As he was getting settled, Naomi stood in front of the evidence board Reed set up. He already had photos of Sean and Dwayne up and other evidence that had been gathered throughout the investigation. Naomi's phone pinged, drawing her attention to her phone. Checking it, she found an email from Wilson Billings. She scanned it. "We just got an official email from Edmon about the memorial service they're going to host for Sean. Looks like it will be taking place tomorrow evening at the Edmon offices."

"I assume I'll be attending with Chief Hughes, but I want you to attend as an Edmon employee."

Naomi wasn't sure why that took her by surprise, but it had. "Why is that? I could ask June if she is going, and if she would want to sit together."

"Curious about how our different vantage points will result in different experiences. Most people assume you've taken time off, but it wouldn't be odd for you to come back for this. We can use it to our advantage."

Naomi folded her arms across her chest. "You think someone who works at Edmon might be involved."

Reed shrugged before sitting down behind his computer. "I'm not one hundred percent sure, but we do know somehow the murderer access to the building after hours. Whether it was an employee, or the system was overridden, like we assume that it was, Edmon has bigger issues on their hands."

"And it wouldn't be hard for someone to figure out his schedule if he was being followed...does MPD have anything that might show he suspected he was being followed?"

Reed shook his head. "No, but that doesn't mean it wasn't happening."

Naomi's eyes made her way back to the board and drifted between Dwayne's photo and Sean's. "I still think the only link is Edmon," she said out loud, but more so to herself. Was Dwayne merely a means to an end? Just a way for the perp to get into the building, or did he have another reason to target Dwayne specifically?

She examined the timeline of events that were laid out on the evidence board. Reed had been working on possible angles that might answer some of the questions they had, but to her, the board looked like a bunch of mismatched puzzle pieces.

"What are we missing?" Naomi mumbled to herself.

Reed's computer beeped. "Motherfucker."

Naomi stole a glimpse at him before she drew her attention back to the board. "What's wrong? What did you find out?"

"First of all, the vial had some sort of agent in it that would have put you to sleep. However, the amount in the dart would have been enough to kill you."

Naomi swallowed hard. She could hear her heart racing, and deep breathing exercises weren't going to cure this.

Her stomach almost dropped to her feet when Reed said, "That's not all. Look at this again." He showed her the photo of the car speeding away from Barry's house. It looked larger on the monitor in front of her versus on her phone. "Does this look familiar?"

Naomi studied it for a few moments. "Can you switch the angle? I want to see the wheels."

Reed did as she asked and switched the angle of the photo

and zoomed in on the back right tires of the car. Naomi was silent before her hands covered her mouth. The words she said came out muffled. She recognized that car.

"I didn't get any of that."

Naomi's hands slowly drifted back down. "That can't be the same car former Officer Tiffany Geller jumped into when she was stalking us on the National Mall."

"It is. The car is registered to PAN, LLC."

As Naomi traveled back to Edmon, just like she had done many times before, her thoughts were scattered. It couldn't be a coincidence that the car that left Barry's house was registered to the same company that her father created. What was it doing there and who was driving it? Was her father involved in this, too? But how? He was sitting in jail after being convicted for murder along with several other charges. Was he controlling all of this from inside of his prison cell?

Naomi tapped her finger on the empty seat next to her along to the soft music playing in the taxi. She and Reed were arriving separately but would be reuniting and going back to his condo afterward. Part of her wished they could have gone together, to be able to lean on him, especially after the bombshell about the car had dropped, but she knew she had to remain steady and calm, even as it felt as if her heart was trying to make its way out of her chest. The sun setting over D.C. captivated her, forcing her eyes to stare out the window. The views she saw, although very familiar, seemed foreign to her. Everything almost blended together as her thoughts were racing a million miles an hour. Could this murder be connected to her?

Naomi thanked and paid the driver after he pulled up in front of Edmon's front doors and stepped out of the car. Once she straightened the black dress she had decided to wear for the occasion, she stepped onto the sidewalk and headed toward the entrance. As she waited for the doors to open, she took the strand of her dark brown hair from behind her ear and readied herself for what could transpire.

Once a person made their way through security and walked past a series of elevators, they would come across two doors that opened into a large vestibule. In the vestibule, there were several doors that all ended in the same place, Edmon's auditorium. Whenever Edmon wanted to bring together a large group of employees, whether it was for meetings, workshops, or an event, they all met there. This space was the perfect place for what Naomi assumed would be a large number of people who would be here to pay their respects to Sean.

Naomi checked her phone and found a text message from June.

June: *I'm standing off to the side near the refreshments outside of the auditorium.*

Naomi: *Okay, I just arrived. See you soon.*

Naomi hoped that would make it somewhat easier to find her but given the amount of people she saw buzzing around the space, she wondered if that would be the case. Most people had decided to wear darker colors to the memorial, blending into the somber mood that had taken over Edmon's headquarters.

Naomi walked into the vestibule and searched for June. It didn't take but a moment to spot her.

When June saw her, she moved through the crowd and pulled her in for a hug. "It feels like forever since we've seen each other in person."

That had been the case. June took off from work after she was rescued and then worked from home. Naomi had visited her once or twice and kept in touch, but it wasn't like seeing her in person at work, and now this.

"How are you doing, June? You look great." But even from personal experience with the demons she faced, Naomi knew that that didn't mean much.

"Some days are better than others, but I'm getting along. How about you?"

"Okay, I've taken a few weeks off from Edmon to have a breather. Everything was getting to be a bit too much."

Naomi was purposefully being vague, not because she didn't trust June, but because there were plenty of eyes and ears around that might be listening in on the conversation.

"I'm happy Edmon was able to pull this together, and that so many people showed up in person, even though the memorial is going to be streamed online."

Naomi nodded as another thought flew through her mind. "Did you know Sean?"

"I saw him in passing every now and then, and we've spoken a few times, but I wouldn't call us friends or anything."

"Did he talk to you about any of the projects he was working on?"

"No, not really. Our conversations were focused around small talk. I didn't know he was a programmer until I read his biography."

It was clear Naomi wasn't going to get any new information out of June. She looked at her phone and pointed to the doors. "The memorial should be starting at any minute. We should probably go inside and sit down."

June nodded, and together, the two women walked into the auditorium and found seats near the middle, closest to an aisle. Many people were still standing, chatting with people as they waited for the program to start.

"You know—"

Naomi's words were cut off as she saw more people filtering in, trying to find their seats. It seemed the organizers were finally telling people it was time for them to sit down.

A couple of minutes later, Naomi turned and found Wilson had entered the auditorium. Chief Hughes followed him into the room. She tracked the two men with her eyes before turning back around toward the end, just to see if Reed was with them. As if summoned by her thoughts, Reed appeared with Detective Finley, but the two men stood in the back of the room. She watched as he scanned the crowd before his eyes landed on her. She slightly nodded, and he gave her a tight smile, trying not to convey their relationship to any prying eyes. Naomi turned her attention back to the front as she wished he would pull her into his arms and hold her.

Wilson Billings walked up to the podium, and an image of Sean appeared with the date of his birth and the date of his death. The crowd quieted down.

"Good evening. I want to thank each and every one of you for coming here to celebrate the life of Sean Barlow. Sean worked at Edmon for seven years and was a star employee in every sense of the word."

As Wilson continued talking, Naomi's eyes drifted until they landed on Barry, who was standing to the left of Wilson. Where Wilson seemed confident and stoic in his appearance, Barry seemed out of sorts. He tugged repeatedly at the collar of his suit and sweat glistened on his forehead under the bright stage lights. Naomi couldn't blame him—he must be under a considerable amount of emotional strain. Her eyes moved further to the left, and she spotted movement behind the curtain. She turned around briefly and looked at Reed, whose eyes were focused straight ahead, but she couldn't tell if he was looking at the same thing she was. It could be anyone making sure the memorial went off without a hitch, but that didn't stop the prickly sensation she felt float across her skin.

Part of her wanted to get up and find out who was behind the curtain. Her thoughts filtered to it potentially being someone who was helping to put this event together and that she should just sit back and pay her respects. But she couldn't stop the feeling that was telling her that this needed to be investigated.

"June, I'm going to go to the bathroom. Do you need anything refreshment wise?"

"I'm ok, thanks though."

Naomi stood up from her seat and as carefully as she could, walked toward the entrance of the auditorium. She looked to see if she could find Reed while she was on her way out, but she found Detective Finley standing by himself. *Where did he go?*

The crowd in the vestibule had diminished considerably due to the program starting in the auditorium. That worked to Naomi's advantage because she was able to easily make her way toward the door that she knew led backstage. When she got close to the door, she found that it was blocked by a man she assumed was a security guard and found Reed standing in front of him. She stopped in her tracks and the sudden movement out of the corner of his eye caused Reed to look over and spot her. In order to not show that they knew each other, she quickly pivoted, acting as if she had gotten lost. She made her way toward the bathroom that was a few feet away and decided that she would talk to Reed about this later.

* * *

"DID you find anything out at the memorial?" Naomi asked as she slipped the heels off of her feet. Finally having her feet free from the constraints that they had been in for a couple of hours, made her sigh in relief.

"Not much." His short response told her he was frustrated by the lack of any potential new information.

"Did you see that movement behind the curtain when Wilson was speaking?"

"I did and I assumed that's why you came into the vestibule."

She had nothing to hide. "Yes, I did. I couldn't get rid of the nagging feeling about something not being right."

"Well Wilson's bodyguard stopped anyone from getting back there and it wasn't like I could shove him aside and cause a scene, so I didn't."

So, he had seen the same thing she did. "Did his bodyguard know who was back there?"

Reed answered, "No, which is worrisome. He did send one

of his guys back there to check it out, but they couldn't find whoever it was."

"Was it a big deal that someone was behind there?"

"Yes. We were trying to restrict who had access to the stage, and everything was set up so even the crew who'd helped put everything together wouldn't be there while Wilson spoke. There was someone back there who had no business being back there. There was some minor concern that someone might try to hurt Wilson."

That caused Naomi to spin around. "Why would someone hurt him?"

"Head of one of the biggest cybersecurity firms the world has ever seen getting injured or killed? Could be an opportunity to get even more media attention. After all, look how much attention Sean's murder is getting, and it continues to grow the longer no one clams responsibility for his death."

That triggered the next thought that had been sitting in the front of her mind all evening.

"Reed, I think I need to speak to my father. After all, the car was registered to—"

"No, you don't."

"Excuse me?" Naomi glared at the man in front of her. She was willing to have a discussion, but there was no way he was telling her what she could and couldn't do.

"Talking to your father again would ruin you. He will try to play some fucked up mind games to get you to do what he wants, and I just don't want to see you get hurt."

He had a good point although his delivery of that point needed work. "Reed, what if this is the only way we can get the person who murdered Sean? It wouldn't hurt to try. After all, the car was registered to PAN, LLC, and we both know who that is." The fact that Morris named a company after her by flipping her initials around still pissed her off.

"I know, but I'm not throwing you completely into harm's way to do it. I can go talk to him."

She scoffed and folded her arms across her body. "He's not going to talk to you."

"You don't know that."

"Reed, what do you think I don't know? You act like you have the answer to everything." Her words were cold, and she narrowed her eyes after Reed didn't respond. Frustration took over, and Naomi walked out of the room and into the main bedroom, doing everything to keep herself from slamming the door in the process.

CHAPTER 13

"Sweetheart, is everything alright?"

Spending time at home, whether it was at her apartment or at her parents' home, always helped Naomi recharge. She was fortunate to be able to see her mother and Logan whenever she wanted, although recently, most of her time was spent with Reed. Childhood memories warmed her soul, providing solace during times of need. Pictures lined the walls of happier times, vacations they had taken together, graduations they attended, events that were celebrated together. Her mother's warm embrace or a pat on the hand from Logan helped comfort her even as an adult.

But this time, things were different. What she wouldn't give to crawl back into her childhood bed and wish everything that happened would fade away. As if nothing had ever occurred.

"I'm—well—no." Naomi averted her eye and grabbed the orange juice sitting in front her. She put the straw in her mouth as she tried to avoid following up with an explanation.

She'd hoped getting breakfast with her mother and step-father would ease some of the stress she was feeling, but she knew she would have to explain what was going, and she didn't want her mother to worry even more than she already was. Jada Porter reached over and placed her only daughter's hand between her own.

"Is this about the murder at your job? That poor man. It's completely understandable why you'd be upset about it. I'm so glad you took time off and don't have to go in, for now."

Naomi and Jada's conversation was interrupted by Logan placing two plates full of bacon, eggs, and pancakes in front of them.

"Thanks, Logan."

"Don't thank me. Thank Simon."

Naomi giggled for what felt like the first time in ages. It felt good to feel something other than worry. Logan joined them at the table with a plate of his own, and they began to eat their breakfast. Logan had been one of the only father figures in her life due to her biological father leaving her and her mother at an early age. She was grateful he had come into their lives when he did and never made her feel as if she was anything other than his daughter.

"Now, please start from the beginning. What's wrong?"

"Well, you all know about what happened with Sean Barlow. I told you, and it's all over the news. So as a result, Reed got called in to help. One of the reasons why I took off work was to help solve the case."

"Wait, really? You're involved now? In this case?"

"Yeah, I am officially helping MPD solve a murder investigation. Actually, there's two murders that have happened which might be connected, but that's not public knowledge, so please don't spread that."

"This has to be very dangerous. It almost reminds me of everything that had happened with Paige a few months ago."

Naomi swallowed hard because her mother unknowingly was right about a connection being between the two. "Yeah, I'm not completely sure this isn't related to that, too."

This revelation caused Jada's mouth to drop wide open. "What do you mean you're not sure it's not connected? Morris is in jail. Yes, they couldn't find Jett, but—"

"While we've been investigating, someone we haven't been able to identify tried to shoot me with a dart that had a substance in it that would have put me to sleep, at the very least."

"Wait, what?" This time, Logan chimed in.

Naomi's eyes found Jada's, and while she had seen her mother get angry over the years, the fury building behind her eyes was the quickest she'd ever seen her get angry. Logan grabbed his wife's hand, and Naomi stood up and gave her a side hug. "Don't worry. Everyone is fine, and we are being safe."

"I know, honey, but that doesn't mean I won't worry, and I know you won't stop until you have an answer."

Naomi smiled before she walked back to her seat and sat down. She wondered if it was worth telling her mother this news, wanting to spare her mother from any further pain caused by her ex-husband. The weariness in her mother's brown eyes led to her second guessing the decision she was about to make, but she did it anyway. Naomi took a deep breath before the words fell out of her mouth. "We saw some surveillance footage, and we were able to figure out the license plate on the car who might have had the person who shot the dart in it. Turns out the car belonged to an organization my father found as a way to antagonize me."

"So, he has someone on the outside who is working with him."

"It seems like, but the only way to figure this out is to go talk to him."

Jada sighed. "I wouldn't be surprised if he's spearheading this to get you to do just that."

She couldn't deny there was a good chance her mother was right. She ran her hands over her face.

"You're not losing it, but I do think going to talk to your father is dangerous, and I don't know how helpful it's going to be."

"Well, we won't know until we try, right? I feel like he holds the key to whatever the heck is going on to these with these murders."

"He might, but I still think talking to Morris is a bad idea. He's going to mess with you, to put it mildly. This is all a game to him. He might still have people that are trying to get you to do what he wants in reference to your job."

The thought had crossed Naomi's mind, but if that was the case, what choice did she have? "It could be, but once again, we won't know until I speak to him. I... I just don't want anyone else to get hurt or die if all of this could have been resolved by talking to Morris."

"How does Reed feel about this?"

"I know he wouldn't be happy about it, but this is my choice, Mom."

Jada stared at her daughter, and Naomi could see the heat

lessening in her eyes. "I completely understand that, but at what cost would it be to you?"

Her mother's warning played over and over in her head, but Naomi couldn't stop the thoughts about this being the only way that this would all come to an end.

Naomi paced back and forth in her room as she debated what to do. She tried to find another solution that would lead to a better result, but there was none. There was only one thing she could do, so she walked over to her desk. She debated finding another way to procrastinate the inevitable but couldn't find one. The only thing that was stopping her from opening the email was herself.

Shaking the doubt from her mind, she sat down at her computer and reread the email that had been burning a hole in her mind since she'd received it months ago. Morris had sent it to one of her spam email accounts, because she assumed he didn't want to alert anyone in prison that he was reaching out, due to her being a victim of his.

Dear N.,

I know I'm the last person you wanted to hear from, but I wanted to send you a quick note, in case you ever wanted to get in touch with me. I'm sure there are plenty of questions you have that have been left unanswered, and I'm more than willing to give you the answers. You can reach me at this email address, and I'll answer, when I'm allowed.

Morris

She put her hands over her face before leaning forward, resting her elbows on her desk. The pit in her stomach grew larger as thoughts about this being the route she had to take to get to the bottom of this case. Although it could be her own anxiety talking, it felt as if the world was on her shoulders once more and this was one of the only opportunities that they had to be able to get a big break in who killed Sean Barlow. She could feel the headache forming, but she resolved to power through it as she tried to not let her anxiety push her down. She knew there was little control that she had of it overall, once it got to a certain point, and she was determined to make sure it didn't get there.

If it got too bad, Naomi knew she had medicine she could grab with ease, and it would calm things down somewhat.

Naomi's finger hovered over the reply button, but for some reason, she couldn't force her finger to click. She put her hand back in her lap and glanced at her phone, which was a couple inches to the left of her computer.

She wanted to call Reed and talk to him about what she was about to do, but she knew he would try to stop her. She was thankful he had dropped her off this morning at her apartment because she would feel even more paranoid thinking about doing this while in his home.

Her mind drifted back to a call that she had with Dr. Evans who talked about how she needed to trust her gut and follow her instincts. Deep down inside, she knew this was the right decision and that she just needed to get it over with.

Her eyes were drawn back to the email, and she closed her

eyes and brought up a new screen and a blank page. She rested her fingers on the keyboard, because she knew dictating her thoughts out loud wouldn't do anything for her anxiety but typing it might be easier.

Dear Morris,

There are a lot of questions I want answers to, and I don't know how much I trust that you'll give them to me. What I want you to do is help me stop someone else from getting hurt. There have been two murders connected to Edmon, and I want to stop all of this, once and for all. If setting up some sort of phone call would be easier for you, we can organize that.

Naomi

A sigh of relief left her lips when she pressed 'send.' She did it. The email was gone, and she debated clicking 'unsend' but stopped herself. This needed to happen.

Naomi didn't want to admit that she was expecting a response immediately, but she was let down by the fact an email didn't pop up in her inbox. At least, her anxiety wasn't through the roof.

She stood up and checked her phone and saw no new notifications. That was until her phone buzzed in her hand.

Reed: *Is everything alright?*

No, everything isn't alright. It feels as if the world is burning from the inside out. If he knew she had contacted her father, he was going to be extremely angry, and she didn't want to deal with that pressure in addition to the pressure she was putting on herself.

Naomi: *Everything is okay. When are you going to be on your way here?*

Reed had gone into the police station for a couple of

hours, and Naomi took it as an opportunity to go back to her apartment to do some quick chores.

Reed: *Should be wrapping things up in about thirty minutes or so. Then I can swing by and pick you up.*

Naomi: *See you then.*

She was putting her phone back down on her desk when she heard a beep from her laptop. There sat an email from Metropolitan Prison. Her stomach was in her throat as she stared at the message in her inbox. Before she could give it too much thought, she clicked on the email and began to read Morris's reply.

I wasn't expecting to hear from you again. I think it's better to discuss this in person.

Naomi's heart dropped. There was no way she could go and visit him in prison. She quickly typed up a response.

A phone call would be fine. We can get this cleared up in ten to fifteen minutes.

He responded almost immediately.

I know, but it would be easier to say everything we need to say in person. You don't owe me anything, and if you never see me again, that's fine.

Now what was she to do?

NAOMI FELT Reed come to bed and turned around, facing toward him. It was hours after he'd picked her up and brought her back to his place. She'd left one of the lamps on in his bedroom so that he would have no issues getting into bed when he came into the room, but now she was thankful to herself for thinking of it because it allowed her to gaze at him.

His body was only covered by the boxer briefs he planned to wear to bed. "Did you finally wrap up everything you needed to?"

"Just finished."

"Looks like someone is turning into me when it comes to working late."

Reed chuckled. "I don't know if I'm turning into you, but there is something that I want to do to you."

"Oh, really? What's that?"

"This."

Reed's lips touched hers gently. Any other thoughts drifted away because all they could think of was being close to one another. They surrendered to the powers of one another's love and that was all that mattered in this moment. His hand cupped her cheek, pulling her in closer to his kiss. His hands migrated down and found a pleasant surprise.

"Oh, I like this," Reed said when his lips were a whisper away from her own as he felt her naked skin under his fingertips.

"I thought you would," she said in return before her lips smashed into his. Without much of a struggle, Naomi flipped Reed over so that she was on top and she took charge. She pulled his boxers off of him before she climbed back on top of his body.

"I like this angle."

"I thought you would," Naomi repeated and ended the laughter that fell from Reed's mouth with a kiss of her own.

When she leaned back and found the part of him that she'd been yearning for and once their bodies connected, both moaned in unison.

"It's your show, cowgirl."

A wicked smile appeared on Naomi's lips knowing that she was in control of their pleasure. She rode him as his hands went from her waist to her breasts, bringing even more euphoria to their union. Naomi had to admit to herself that this might be one of the best ideas she ever had. Naomi sped up and when Reed started moving his hips, she could have screamed in pleasure. Their in-sync movements caused both of them to get closer and closer to an explosion of ecstasy.

Naomi cried out when she reached the point of no return but didn't stop until Reed met her there. When she fell on his chest, she trembled. The softness of his fingertips brushing along her back as he caressed her caused goosebumps to appear on her golden-brown skin.

When she regained her strength however many minutes later, she rolled off of him, but tucked into his side. She stretched and gave Reed a sassy smile. "There's plenty more where that came from."

"Don't I know it."

Naomi shook her head and reached over to grab her phone. She saw she had several missed calls from June and a couple of text messages.

June: Hey, are you there?

June: Please call me as soon as you see this.

Naomi raised an eyebrow as she called June, making sure to keep her screen off because she and Reed were undressed.

"Hello?" June's voice sounded different...almost as if she were upset.

"Hey, June."

"Oh my gosh, there you are, Naomi. Have you checked our team chat? I've been trying to call you for the last twenty minutes. Doug's been hurt, and he's in the hospital."

CHAPTER 15

Naomi and Reed raced into the hospital. Fear crawled down Naomi's spine because the only information she had on Doug's condition was what June had said. There had been no reports from MPD about another person from Edmon being hurt. That could be for a number of reasons, but it didn't help Naomi's state of mind.

It wasn't hard for them to get past the hospital's security due to Reed's badge, and they received their guest passes and were directed to take the elevator to the seventh floor. Once they arrived on the seventh floor, Naomi walked up to a kiosk and showed her guest badge. Doug's room number quickly popped up. While she was doing this, Reed sent a message to Detective Finley, telling him everything he currently knew, and that he might be needed at the hospital to take an official statement. He closed out the message by saying he believed this was connected to Sean Barlow/Edmon before pressing 'send.' When he looked up, Naomi was a couple of feet ahead of him, walking to what he assumed was Doug's hospital room.

When they reached the room, Naomi took a deep breath and walked in because the door wasn't closed. She could have screamed in relief when she laid eyes on the man lying in the bed but refrained due to the location they were in. In the perspective of a non-medical professional, Doug didn't look too bad. Of course, that didn't mean he didn't have any internal injuries or any longer-term effects from what happened to him, but the most important thing to her was that he looked very much alive.

Thoughts had flown through her head on the way to the hospital about what condition he would be in when she saw him. His eyes were closed when they entered, and he looked a little paler than normal, with some bruising on his body and a bandage around his left arm. The only noise that could be heard in the room was coming from the television, as some light murmurs came from a sitcom on the small screen hanging from the wall opposite his bed. Naomi assumed he was hooked up to several machines monitoring his condition, but no noise could be heard. Reed closed the door behind them.

Doug must have heard the couple enter his room because he opened his eyes. "Naomi, what are you doing here? Heck, I don't know what I'm doing here." He adjusted his body and winced.

"Oh my gosh, Doug." Naomi rushed to his bedside. "Are you okay?"

"I think so. I did get slashed with a knife, and I have a few bruised ribs and some cuts, due to me getting really kicked in the torso, but I'll survive. Hoping to be out of here in the next day or so. I can recover from this type of condition at home."

Naomi looked at Reed and knew they were thinking the

same thing. The attacker had a knife, which immediately drew a connection to Sean Barlow's murder. Only thing was, the murderer had left the knife at the scene so was this the same person, or a copycat?

"Thank goodness whoever attacked you didn't do more damage."

Doug glanced at Reed before closing his eyes for a moment. Reed walked closer to Doug's bed and placed a hand on Naomi's shoulder. Naomi looked up at him before looking back at Doug.

"We can come back, if you want to rest some."

"No, I'm okay to talk now. Maybe not for very long but talking now is fine. I assume my girlfriend will be here soon. She was away for the weekend when one of my doctors called her and told her what happened."

"Okay, we'll make this quick," said Reed, who chimed in for the first time since he and Naomi entered the room. "Did you see the person who did this to you?"

Doug shook his head. "No, but I was surprised he didn't try to attack me more with the knife once he got me down on the ground. Instead, they continued kicking and punching me in the torso. They could have easily killed me yet didn't."

"Did you see anything that could give you any inclination as to who they were? Even if you didn't see the person's face?"

Doug glanced to his left for a moment before looking at Reed. "I thought it could be a man but didn't want to assume. Wore dark colored clothes during the attack."

"Where were you when the attack occurred?" Naomi asked.

"A block away from Edmon headquarters. I went in to grab a hard drive that had a few files I needed on it. I'd left at the office when everything with Sean happened, and I thought I would be in and out because we didn't need to be escorted into the building anymore. I was attacked from behind."

"Did the person steal something from you? Was it an attempted mugging?"

Doug shook his head slightly. "They didn't steal any money or anything. I do have a hard drive that is missing."

"What's on it?" Naomi held her breath as she waited for his response.

"Mostly files pertaining to some of my projects."

Naomi was leaning more into the copycat theory. "Was it anything super important? Is it anything that isn't backed up?"

"It wasn't, but clearly the person who put me here didn't know that. I've already reported that it's missing to Edmon. Haven't talked to the police yet."

"Well, they should be here soon," Reed chimed in.

Doug yawned and closed his eyes, giving Naomi cues that he was fading. It was best for him to get some rest, and she peered up at Reed once more and gestured with her head that they should leave.

She stood up from where she had been sitting at his bedside. "Doug, we're going to leave you alone to rest, but I assume MPD will be here soon to take your official statement."

All he did was nod, acknowledging he had heard her. She and Reed walked toward the door when Doug clearing his throat stopped them mid-step.

"Oh, one more thing." The couple turned around. "The person said there'll be no other warnings for you, Naomi."

"Wait what?" Naomi walked back over to Doug's bedside.

"Yes. I didn't recognize the voice or anything, but the voice was deep. The whole fight was a bit of a blur."

Naomi swallowed hard. It freaked her out that someone, once again, was gunning for her. The reason why Paige had been kidnapped was due to their relationship, and now Doug's attack had been a result of him being her boss.

A knock on the door stopped the conversation from proceeding any further. Reed opened it and walked in Detective Finley. He greeted everyone in the room, and just as he finished talking, Doug yawned again.

"I came here to take a statement from you, but if you need to rest, we can do it when you wake up."

Doug shook his head. "Let's get it over with."

"How about I tell Detective Finley what you told us, and then you can fill in any gaps? He should have some background knowledge of this before he starts.".

Doug agreed, and Naomi and Reed related the information that Doug had told them to Detective Finley.

"Naomi, I hope you don't take this lightly. If you need some sort of protection—"

"It's taken care of," Reed said as his hand rested on the small of her back. He looked at Naomi. "We should probably head out."

Naomi nodded and turned to Doug to give him a small wave. As the couple exited the room, Naomi felt as if her entire world had shifted.

CHAPTER 16

"This can't continue."

Doug's warning was the big elephant in the room, and there was no escaping it. His words ran on repeat in Naomi's mind, and if there had been any question before about whether or not she was connected to the case, it should be answered now.

Reed agreed. "Which means we need to figure out who is responsible for this as soon as possible."

Naomi knew there was a potential way to get the information they needed but bit her tongue. She knew the answer wouldn't be popular with Reed, and as soon as she mentioned it, it would be as if a bomb exploded.

"Are we basically at a dead end? Or is Detective Finley keeping things from you and they are working behind the scenes on an angle?"

"I don't think he would do that. We all have the same goal here, and it's not as if I would be hindering his career progression. Plus, he's not the type of guy."

Bringing up her father was still bubbling underneath the

surface. It was a path they hadn't explored, and one that could prove to be dangerous. The end results were unpredictable, but if Naomi had to be honest with herself, it was a path she was willing to take.

What he didn't know was she could and did easily get in contact with Morris without going through official channels. Keeping this from Reed was making her feel guilty given the gravity of the situation. She had started thinking about that email more and more as the connection to Edmon grew stronger and stronger.

She watched Reed walk back-and-forth in his living room, clearly a habit he'd picked up from spending time with her. Naomi's instinct was telling her that she had a key to this puzzle and tying it to her father would be the beginning of the end for this whole operation.

"Reed."

Reed stopped his movements, pausing right to look at Naomi. She knew what she was about to say was going to set up a chain reaction, and she tried to briefly prepare herself for what was about to come.

"Reed, we need to talk to my father."

His eyes widened for a moment before they narrowed into slits, and his jaw tightened as his lips thinned. "No, we don't. There is nothing you need to hear from that man, Naomi. He's a manipulative bastard, and I don't want you anywhere near him."

She could have predicted this would be his reaction, but she had to try to convince him it was important to take this risky step, if it meant saving more lives.

"Reed, he's got information we need, and you know it!"

"Fine, then let somebody else go collect it. You don't need

to be the one to do it. Hell, I'll go do it, but you need to stay the hell away from him." Reed's hands curled into fists at his sides.

Naomi huffed. She wasn't some fragile doll who couldn't handle herself. Besides, she knew something he didn't, and the fact he was treating her like a child was starting to piss her off. "Morris isn't going to talk to anyone besides me. We've crossed this ground before, Reed. He's not going to talk to you or anyone other than me."

Her response triggered something in Reed. His heated stare burned, and it wasn't with lust. There was intense anger in his blue eyes, turning them stormy, and it was directed right at her—not at Morris or the situation—but directly at her.

"What did you do, Naomi?" His voice held an edge to it. "Did you contact him?" he accused. His breath was coming rapidly. He was seething with anger, and it was pulsing out of him.

There was no way she could lie to Reed, and she wouldn't. She met his gaze defiantly. "I did."

The fury flared brighter in his blue eyes. "You had better be joking. The last time you spoke to this man, he tried to kill me and Paige! He is a monster, Naomi! He was blackmailing you! How can you even consider—"

Naomi cut him off. "I'm not doing this to make peace with him, Reed! I'm trying to stop more people from getting hurt! Don't you see? Doug is in the hospital because of me. This is my fault! Talking to Morris could keep other people from getting hurt!"

Reed turned and stalked away from her, before whirling,

finger raised. "The man is a manipulative liar! A monster! He's not going to help you! Why can't you see that?"

His voice boomed around her, and her stance changed from worried to angry. "You don't think I know that? I had to deal with his rejection of me for years, long before you came into the picture, so I don't need you to tell me who or what he is!"

Once the words left her mouth, she could see the change in Reed's expression, one that went from extremely pissed off to shutting down and cold.

"Really." A muscle twitched in his jaw as he stared at her, his face basically blank, his emotions shut off.

"Look, this isn't something I expected to deal with on top of everything else. I'm just going to go." Her face burned.

"Maybe you should."

Naomi wavered, worried she'd pushed him too far, but he'd done the same to her and she knew she was right. "Reed, maybe we both need some space and time, because this has all gotten to be a bit too much."

He took a breath, then said, "I'll take you home."

She could still feel the disappointment and rage coming off him. His back was rigid, and his fists were clenched like he was ready to hit something. She knew he'd never hit her, but he was like a caged tiger right then, and she wasn't sure she wanted to be trapped in a car with him at that moment. "No, I can call a car."

He nodded and walked away from her, heading into the kitchen, leaving her on her own.

With tears filling her eyes, Naomi walked out of Reed's condo, not knowing if that would be the last time she'd see him.

* * *

Once she was safely in the backseat of the car, Naomi shed some tears. Things had gone the way she thought they would, but she wished they hadn't. She didn't want to get into a fight with Reed or ruin what they had, but she knew what she'd said needed to be out in the open.

She stared at her phone, willing it to ring or to see a text from Reed, but there wasn't one. Maybe he needed time to cool off, which was understandable. Part of her wanted to ask the driver of this car to turn around and take her back to Reed's condo, but she knew she had to stand her ground. Naomi knew in the end she had done what was right to save potentially more lives, and that was something she might need to just live with.

She opened her email app and stared at the message from Morris. The message was now haunting her, and there was a potential chance he'd inadvertently ruined one of the best things she had going for her right now. But that had been her choice, one she hoped she soon wouldn't regret. This didn't include the damage he had done and continued to do to her mental health. With a sharp pain forming in her head, Naomi took a deep breath and typed out a message to Morris.

I'll make arrangements to come for a visit.

CHAPTER 17

Naomi's knee bounced up and down as she tried not to think about what she was about to do. The pep talk she had given herself before she arrived, had been thrown out the window. Nothing she was doing would stop her nerves from climbing. The only thing keeping her in this seat was the fleeting hope this might save someone else from getting hurt or killed. There would be no more of that on her watch if she could prevent it.

When Naomi arrived, she went through security and signed in, indicating who she was and who she was trying to see. The process hadn't been as terrible as she was expecting, but she made sure to keep her expectations low, just in case.

Metropolitan Prison was a state-of-the-art prison with high-tech facilities. The building had bright lights and looked immaculate, and had been done as a way to improve the infrastructure of many of the nation's facilities. It did help her feel more comfortable in the location, but nothing could take away the nerves she felt about seeing her father again in person.

"Ms. Porter?"

Naomi looked up from the wall she had been staring at and glanced at the woman behind the desk. "Yes?"

"This security guard is going to take you a room to meet with Mr. Washington." A man in a white shirt appeared next to the desk and waved her toward him.

Naomi swallowed hard as she smoothed her hands down the dark slacks she had chosen to wear today. She followed the security guard through a white door and down a long white hall. The security guard wasn't what she would call pleasant, but he wasn't rude either. He didn't try to speak to her, and she was admittedly thankful for that. Having to make small talk during a circumstance that Naomi had already chalked up to being awkward wasn't her idea of having a good time.

They reached another door, and the security guard opened it without delay. The room contained a large glass window that split the room into two. A table and a couple of chairs were on her side of the wall, while just a chair was on the other. Naomi didn't know she could request a room like this and was thankful it was provided for her, because she didn't want to be any closer to Morris than she needed to be.

"Session will be for twenty minutes, and all you need to do is ask Simon to allow you to turn on the speaker in front of you or to turn it off. If you want to end it early, click the button underneath the table."

Naomi nodded and walked over to the chair before sitting down. She found the button with her fingers but didn't press it.

"Do you need anything? Water?"

Naomi shook her head and whispered, "Thank you." Her voice wavered slightly, and she took another deep breath.

"I'll be just on the other side of this door until your session ends."

"Okay," Naomi said, and soon, she was left alone to face the person who had helped shape her into the person she was today, because of his absence.

Naomi tapped her foot as she waited for Morris to be led into the room, trying to keep her nervous energy from consuming her and buzzing around the room. She wished she had her phone. It would have kept her entertained while the seconds slowly ticked by, but due to the rules at the prison, no electronics were allowed. She'd left her phone in the car that she rented, completely severing her connection with the outside world until she left the facility.

A door on the other end of the window opened, and Naomi's heart rate increased tenfold. This was the moment of truth.

She watched as another security guard brought Morris Washington into the room. Naomi tried to silence the pounding of her heartbeat in her ears, and mostly succeeded. The man in front of her looked different than the one she remembered seeing in the kitchen of the home where Paige and June were kept. He'd lost weight since his sentencing, and the circles under his eyes had grown darker and deeper.

Once he was settled at the chair in front of her and the security guard left the room, he gave her a small smile, one she couldn't return.

"Simon, microphone on." A small red light appeared next to the speaker, letting her know that Simon had honored her quest. She nodded curtly, trying to conceal her own nerves. "Hi, Morris."

"Hi, Naomi. It's good to see you."

She fought against her own instinct to throw back a minor insult at him. "Let's get down to business, shall we? What do you know about the recent events that have occurred at Edmon?"

"I'm not sure what you mean."

"Cut the bullshit. You know about the Sean Barlow murder, at the very least, because it's been all over the news, and I mentioned that there were two murders connected to Edmon. What. Do. You. Know. About. Them?"

Morris studied her for a few moments before speaking. "It's a convoluted story."

"Well, I'm here for you to spell it out for me. This could have taken place over the phone, but you want to meet here, and I did as you asked. So, tell me everything that you know." Naomi resolved not to give Morris an inch more gratitude than he deserved.

Morris leaned closer to his speaker. "I didn't have anything to do with Sean Barlow's murder. I didn't ask for him to be killed, but I'm not surprised he's dead."

He had Naomi's full and undivided attention. "Why aren't you surprised he was murdered?"

"Because he was doing too much and he should have kept quiet."

"You've lost me," Naomi said in a huff. She was teetering close to the edge of snapping due to Morris's purposeful vagueness. She pushed down Reed's words about Morris just wanting to toy with her.

"Sean was killed because he knew too much. He outlived

his purpose for finding out about where Cyber Edge is because he was getting ready to talk. Or at least that's what people are whispering."

Naomi's eyes darted to the door, wondering if the security guards could hear what was being said. Then again, it wasn't like they had much of a choice anyway. "So, the same information I was supposed to gather for you, someone was trying to get Sean to deliver to them?"

Morris nodded. "The person I was working for isn't the only one after the information in that file."

His answer surprised Naomi, but it made sense. If this information in this file was as valuable as he thought it was, then having more than one person trying to find it was understandable.

"Who did you work for?"

"It's best you don't know that information."

"Morris, I swear—"

"Naomi, you're already in too deep with this."

Naomi slammed her fists down on the table and stood up. She didn't care who heard her, or if she was causing a scene because the anger coursing through her body had taken over every emotion. "I've literally done nothing. I've lived my life the best way I knew how, and I keep getting thrown into shit that I barely understand. I've had enough, and I want some answers now!"

She could see Morris weighing his options. "Sean made the mistake of thinking that he could gain the upper hand on the person that hired him, and it came back to bite him."

Hired him? For both his job and the server project? Her thoughts traveled back to her conversation with Barry. No, it couldn't be...

"Wilson Billings, CEO of one of the biggest companies the world has ever seen, is involved in this?"

Morris shrugged, letting his statement hang between them. Naomi's suspicions increased tenfold.

"Why should I believe that you're telling the truth? You have no problem lying when it benefits you, no matter the situation."

Naomi could tell her comment stung him based on the look on his face. It only lasted for a flash of a second, but Morris's mouth fell open and his expression went slack before his normal look of indifference appeared back on his. "You don't have much of a choice, do you?"

Naomi knew he was right. She had nothing else to go on. "Continue."

"Do you remember when we were standing in the kitchen, just before the police burst through the door?"

Naomi nodded, but didn't say anything.

"I told you that I wasn't good enough for you. Hopefully, this will do something to rectify the damage that I've done. Look out for a call that you should be receiving from an unknown number in a couple of days."

He must have hit his own button because although Naomi didn't hear anything, the security guard that escorted him into the room waltzed back in, ready to take Morris back to his cell.

When Morris was led out of the room, Naomi took a deep breath and exhaled. She was directed on how she could reach her rental car and once she was out of Metropolitan Prison, she did the thing she had been wanting to do most: she cried.

CHAPTER 18

Sitting under a blanket out on her balcony did little to warm Naomi, even in the dead of summer. She was cradling the glass of wine she'd retrieved from the kitchen fifteen minutes ago, and she couldn't even bother to bring the glass up to her lips. Naomi watched as cars moved slowly down the streets of D.C., as people drove away from their jobs during rush hour to their homes. She spent so much time out on this balcony that it had seen her at her best and at her worse. At this moment, she didn't know if this was one of the closest times she'd been to hitting rock-bottom.

A slight headache that formed after she had returned from a visit with her father was still present, even though this soothing environment surrounded her, and it was hours later.

Naomi had wondered if Sean's murder was in any way connected to her, along with Doug's attack. The subsequent warning that he had been told to pass onto her almost confirmed it. While she had the answer to one question, a whole lot more had formed as a result. What did this person want from her? And if it wasn't her father behind all this chaos, who was it?

Between the current state of things with Reed, visiting her biological father, and working on a murder investigation, everything seemed to be upside down. The one constant that she'd had over the last few months was Reed. Now, not having him in her corner during a tumultuous time cut her to her core. They'd both been there to reach for the other as he'd recovered physically from the ordeal with her father and the mental toll everything took on her. Now they were apart, and it felt odd. When her phone buzzed, she looked down and found a message from Reed. Her thoughts must have summoned him.

Reed: *I want to talk about what happened whenever you're ready.*

Naomi debated replying before shaking her head. This was one of many texts she'd received from Reed over the last couple of days, and she felt guilty about the way things had transpired between them. There was nothing more she wanted to do than to fall into his arms and have him tell her everything would be okay, but right now she knew where her focus needed to lie. Deep down, she knew she didn't need to respond to him right now, if she didn't want to. It didn't help that she didn't know what to say.

"I haven't seen you do this in a long time."

Naomi over her shoulder and found Paige standing in the doorway. "How long have you been there?"

"Long enough to see you sitting out here and notice that you haven't taken a sip of your wine, and I know that's not like you. You've been staring off into the sunset. What's wrong?"

Naomi knew there was no use in keeping this to herself. "It's just a lot going on. Reed and I had a fight, this murder investigation. Oh, and I saw my father today. Morris."

Paige was next to Naomi in no time, pulling the only other chair on the balcony closer to her. She sat down next to her best friend and roommate and grabbed one of her hands.

"You have a lot on your plate. Let's start with M—Morris. How'd it go?"

Naomi was relieved that was all she said. Anything other than this question might have sent her over the edge. It didn't go unnoticed that Paige had said Morris's name. She hadn't been able to say it after her kidnapping, but she'd told Naomi that her therapist was helping her get to the point of where saying his name wouldn't cause her to second guess herself or immediately spiral into thoughts of her kidnapping.

"I…don't know? My nerves were a mess, and the only reason I went to see him was because I thought he might be connected with Sean Barlow and Dwayne Clearance's murders and be behind the reason why Doug was attacked."

"Did he have any answers for you?"

Naomi shrugged. "He said he had nothing to do with it, and someone would contact me to help me. No timeframe on when that will happen, though."

Paige squeezed her hands. "I have a bad feeling about this."

"You and me both, but I don't want anyone else to get hurt, so this is a risk I'm willing to take."

"Even if it costs you your life? You know the people your father deals with are dangerous, and now it seems as if he is pushing you into the lion's den to face whatever monster is on the other side."

Naomi couldn't deny Paige's assumption. Morris could

have been royally screwing her over, and who knew how much damage it could cause. But if there was even a small chance of stopping anyone else from getting hurt, she was going to take it.

"I know. And don't get me wrong, that does worry me."

"Well, if you need me, you know I'm always here, right?"

Paige's words nearly broke the mask Naomi had put on to hide her feelings. The headache she was dealing with picked up steam, and she sighed. She slipped her hand out of Paige's and put her wine glass down on the small table between them.

"Thanks."

"Now, tell me, do I need to go kick Reed's ass? What did he do?"

Naomi smiled, glad that Paige automatically assumed Reed was the one in the wrong. "Honestly, nothing I wasn't expecting. It's just this situation. We'll figure it out, or not. Right now, well, I just need to do what I feel is right."

"Is there anything I can do?"

Naomi shook her head. "No, but I appreciate you being here."

Paige stood up, placing a hand on Naomi's shoulder. "I'm going to head inside."

"I'll be in there in a minute."

Paige gave a small smile before she turned around and walked back inside. When Naomi was by herself again, she leaned back on my chair and closed her eyes. That seemed to help the headache.

Naomi spent some more time taking in the sunset before she grabbed her things and headed back into her apartment. She felt bad tossing her wine down the drain, but while it looked appetizing before she'd poured it, it didn't now. She wandered into her bedroom and decided that a warm relaxing shower was in order.

When she stepped into the shower, Naomi programmed her shower to her normal 102 degrees before moving under the spray. Usually, she asked Simon to play the news while she showered, but today, she decided to change things up.

"Simon, please play soft music, lower the lights, and add a touch of eucalyptus scent to the bathroom."

Simon did as she asked, and she sighed. This was a spa experience, and the only thing that was missing was a long soak in the tub. She didn't think about all of the things she needed to do—the case, her fight with Reed, or her father. She tried to focus on putting her stressors on the back burner, at least for right now.

When she stepped out of the shower, she felt rejuvenated as she dried herself and ran through her after shower routine. Once she was in her sweats, Naomi checked her phone and found a message.

Unknown Number: *Naomi Porter.*

Naomi raised an eyebrow at the message.

Naomi: *Who wants to know?*

Unknown Number: *Morris asked me to contact you.*

Naomi's heart jumped into her throat. This was the person she'd been waiting for?

Naomi: *I'm Naomi. Who is this?*

Unknown Number: *Meet me at M St and 4th St NW in 2 hours.*

Naomi: *No, who are you?*

Naomi waited a few beats to see if she'd get a response, but there was none, leaving plenty of questions hanging in front of her. She had a decision to make, and the heaviness of it weighed on her. She vowed to come up with a decision about what she was going to do sooner rather than later.

CHAPTER 19

Naomi gave herself one more glance in the mirror before walking into the hallway. Her ensemble was all black from the hoodie she'd selected, just in case there was a chill in the air, down to her jeans and sneakers. She pulled her hair back into a ponytail, thankful the headache she was suffering from had subsided just before she'd gotten the mysterious text. She grabbed her phone and strolled out of her room.

"Where are you going? I thought you were staying home for the night."

Naomi looked over at Paige who was sitting on the couch reading a book. Naomi was somewhat shocked she wasn't working, but everyone needed to take a break sometimes.

"I was, but I need to handle something."

Paige raised an eyebrow, clearly not believing the vagueness of Naomi's comment. Paige glanced at her phone before turning back to Naomi. "This late at night?"

Naomi nodded, before a thought popped into her head.

"Listen, I'm not sure how long I'll be gone, but can you track my location?"

Paige sat up and put the phone down next to her. "What are you getting yourself into? Can I come with you?"

Naomi put a hand up, gesturing for Paige to not come any closer. "I don't think that's the best idea, but if you don't hear from me every twenty minutes or so, can you call the police?"

"Now, Naomi—"

"Please, Paige, this is something that I need to do alone, and I'll let you know what happens when I come back. But if you don't hear from me, promise me you'll call the police?"

As the words left Naomi's mouth, her throat felt dry. Reality was setting in as Naomi had no idea what she was walking into, with little to no backup in case something bad happened. She needed Paige to promise this one small thing which could mean life or death.

"You know I will. Since I can't stop you from going, can you promise me that you'll be safe?"

"Yes, I will," Naomi said, although she knew that wasn't a promise she could guarantee. She called a car from her phone and walked over to Paige, who'd been staring at Naomi from the couch. She leaned over to give her a hug, and it didn't go unnoticed that Paige was hugging her tighter than usual. Naomi shook slightly as she pulled back, doing her best not to show the gesture had affected her. "I'll be back soon."

"Okay."

Naomi could feel Paige's eyes burning a hole in her back as she walked to their front door. She wanted to turn around and walk back to her room and curl up underneath the covers, but that wasn't feasible right now. The door closed, forcing her feet to move down the stairs. When she reached the lobby, Naomi's focus was drawn to her phone. She checked to make sure she still had a few minutes before the car arrived before looking up and toward the front desk. She was happy to find Ann standing there.

"Good evening, Naomi. Everything okay?"

Naomi nodded, not trusting her words to convince her that she wasn't lying. "How are you?"

"I'm doing well. Let me know if you need anything, and I hope you enjoy the rest of your evening."

"Thanks. You too."

Naomi was relieved. Normally, she loved talking to Ann for a little while, if she was coming back to her apartment or leaving, but right now, just the simple social interaction proved to be too stressful.

With a small wave, Naomi turned around and walked toward the exit. She looked down again and saw that the driver was a block away. She'd thought about taking the Metro, but that would just give her more time to sit there and wallow in her thoughts. Once she was settled in the backseat of the car, her phone buzzed, and she saw that there was a message from Reed. She didn't bother reading the message, instead choosing to text Paige.

Naomi: I'm on my way to M St. and 4th NW.

Paige: Okay. I'm watching on my end.

Naomi smiled for the first time all night. She was so thankful to have a friend who was willing to do this for her, no questions asked.

The drive to the location was short, in part due to it being after rush hour in Washington, D.C. Dread crept into her mind the closer they got to their destination. She was walking into a potentially dangerous situation and didn't know what the end result of this evening would be. That unknown painted a dark cloud over her. When the car pulled up on the corner of the intersection, Naomi's heart leapt into her throat.

"Here you are, miss."

"Uh, thank you." Naomi scrambled to get out of the car.

"Do you want me to wait here? It's awfully dark on this block."

His description was correct. The light that would normally illuminate this corner of the intersection was out, and the distance between it and the next closest one was too far away to cast more light this way.

"I'll be okay, thanks," Naomi said that more herself than for him. She'd wanted to ask him to stay until whomever this was showed up, but she also didn't want to spook them and ruin any chance she had at gathering more information.

The driver nodded, and once she closed the door, he took off. Soon, the only thing she could see was his brake lights in the distance.

Silence surrounded her on all sides as she looked down the street to see if there was any type of vehicle approaching. There was nothing, not a soul to be found. Naomi pulled out her phone to see if she had a text from the unknown number but found none. She decided to wait five more minutes, and if no one showed up, she'd either call a car or take the Metro home.

When it was down to a minute to go, a black car slowly drove up and stopped in front of her. For a second, she wondered if the driver might try to pull a fast one, but the only thing that happened was that the driver's side window rolled down. The driver's face was obscured by the shadows. "Get in."

*N*ot having much of a choice if she wanted to find out the answers to the questions that haunted her, Naomi walked around to the passenger's side of the car and got in.

"Put this on."

Naomi turned and found a woman sitting in the driver's seat. In her hand, was a blindfold Naomi recognized as being one that once it is on your face, there was no way you could see anything unless you click a small button that removes it from your face.

"And if I say no?" Naomi raised an eyebrow at her.

"Then we don't go anywhere, and you're welcome to go home."

The underlying message was Naomi wouldn't get the answers she needed if she didn't follow these directions. It was also clear the driver didn't want her knowing the path they were taking to get to wherever they were going. She picked that up loud and clear. Naomi hesitated, staring at the blindfold in her hand.

"So, are we leaving or are you staying?"

Her question hung in the air, as Naomi weighed the pros and cons. After a quick debate with herself, Naomi grabbed the blindfold and saw the woman smirk as Naomi put it on. Once it was covering her eyes and Naomi pressed the button, she was surrounded by total darkness. The darkness heightened her senses as the car cruised to a destination unknown. Having a blindfold on raised Naomi's anxiety levels, because she felt as if she had to put trust into a woman whose name she didn't even know. Not to mention, it was Morris who connected the two of them.

Finally, the woman spoke. "What? You're not going to ask questions? Try to figure out what is going on? Do you regularly get in the car with complete strangers who ask you to put on blindfolds?"

"No, but I was wondering if the answers to my questions would cause me to panic more."

"Understandable. Completely reasonable given the circumstances."

Her words didn't instill confidence in Naomi. "Who are you? Why did you text me and Wherever are we going?"

"Name's Molly, and I'm here because you talked to Morris."

Distrust ran throughout her entire body, and everything was telling her that she should bolt out of the moving vehicle. Yet, she was determined to find out what this was all about. "You're going to have to give me more than that. I'm almost positive that everyone involved in this situation, including the people who are dead, know more about this that I do."

Molly braked at what Naomi assumed was a stop light.

"Morris thought it would be easier to show you, rather than to tell you, and that's what we're going to do."

Molly sped off again into the night, and Naomi resisted the urge to press the button on her blindfold and check her phone to make sure Paige was still able to track her movements. But she didn't want to call unnecessary attention to it. She wished she had been able to, at the very least, time their drive to have an idea of where she might be.

After a few more minutes, Naomi asked, "Where are we going?"

"Right here. You can remove the blindfold."

As she said that, Naomi pressed the button and pulled the blindfold from her face. It didn't take long for her eyes to adjust to the newfound light because it was nighttime. She caught a glimpse of some houses before Molly navigated the car into what looked like an underground garage. The brief moment Naomi saw the homes caused a flashback to fly through her mind. "This reminds me of the house where we found Paige," she mumbled.

"It is pretty similar, but it's more than meets the eye. Come on."

Naomi looked around the garage and immediately thought there was no way she had signal down here, so if Molly invited her up into whatever building, this garage was underneath. "Is this your way of getting me alone so you could kill me? I'm suspicious of anyone who Morris deals with."

"Given what I heard happened a few months ago with the whole kidnapping thing, I'm not surprised by your distrust. I had nothing to do with that because I wasn't assigned to it."

"Assigned?"

"More on that later. Come on, we need to get upstairs

now. There is someone you need to meet, and a few things you need to see."

"Do I get to know who I'm supposed to be meeting?"

Molly smirked at Naomi before unlocking the car door. "Nah. We can keep the surprises rolling."

Naomi almost groaned, but instead, she followed Molly's lead and opened her car door. Both women stepped out of the car and walked toward a dark red door. The chipped paint gave off the appearance that this building wasn't kept up as much as some of the other buildings in D.C. That was until Molly opened the door and led Naomi to another door down a hall.

"Um. What the hell did I just walk into?"

Naomi's question was an understatement. The hallway Molly had just led her along was nondescript, but once they reached another door at the end, Naomi's. mouth fell open as she was blown away by what lay on the other side.

It was as if she'd walked into a high-tech conference room. The black screen that showcased nothing at the moment reminded her somewhat of what she had seen in Chief Hughes's office. However, if her instincts were correct, the electronics in here might outpace what was currently in his office.

Naomi walked around and found there was not just one high-powered computer but at least four. Based on the maps Naomi could see, each one seemed to focus on a quadrant in Washington, D.C. She walked over to the northwest quadrant and found a map had a small red dot on it. Naomi was able to deduce it was Edmon headquarters, due to the familiar cross streets. Thoughts swirling through her mind as she wondered if this was a trap Morris had set up. It was clear whoever was behind this, also had their sights set on Edmon, both figuratively and literally.

Everything in the room was starting to overwhelm Naomi as more questions appeared in her mind instead of answers. "When am I going to be told what the hell is going on?"

"Right now."

A new voice Naomi didn't recognize said the words, causing both her and Molly to turn around. A woman dressed in a green power suit walked out of a secret door. Her red glossy hair was pulled into a tight bun at the nape of her neck. "Genevieve Platt. It's nice to meet you, Naomi."

Genevieve held her hand out for Naomi to shake, but Naomi just stared at it before she replied, "I would say it's nice to meet you, but given the circumstances, I'd be telling a lie." The bite in her words told everyone in the room she wasn't kidding about that.

"Makes sense." Genevieve took her hand back before she turned to Molly. "How much does she know?"

"I doubt much of anything, based on the questions she was asking."

Genevieve nodded. "Well, it's time to do some explaining, especially since Morris wanted you to know."

"Does Morris work for you?"

"Yes, he does. As does Molly. Even Jett was working for me, at one point."

The very mention of Jett's name had Naomi on edge. "So, you're the one who told Morris he should kidnap my best friend and blackmail me into getting the data from Cyber Edge."

"That's not true at all. I'm the one who assigned him to the case. It's up to my agents, if you will, to choose how they want to achieve the objective."

"Are you like the FBI or something?"

Genevieve chuckled. "No. The reason why Morris works for me is because he owes me for helping to wipe the debt he owed to other people. I knew his potential and figured it was to my advantage to take him in and bring his experience to our team."

"So, there's more than just you, Morris, and Molly?"

"Way more."

"What is it that you want with the Cyber Edge file?"

"At first? My goal was to get the data inside of it and sell it. It could be worth billions. Now, I want to protect it."

Naomi still didn't trust any of this, but she was happy someone was finally telling her what was going on.

"Protect it from what?"

"From those that wish to steal it, one of whom is in your very own company."

As much as Naomi didn't want to hear the name, she had to confirm it. "I assume you're talking about Wilson Billings."

"Yeah. That asshole."

To Naomi, it almost seemed as though Genevieve had a personal hatred for Wilson. She wasn't sure if Genevieve realized how her expression had changed once Naomi had mentioned his name. Her eyes grew tight, her face turned slightly red, and her lips curled. Naomi almost expected her to growl or launch into a tirade about him, but she didn't.

"Do you have some history?"

"Oh, do we have history. He's my ex-husband."

"Wait a minute. Hold on. Were two people kidnapped and two people killed because you and Wilson have some underlying issues with one another? Is this a pissing contest?"

Genevieve scoffed. "Hardly. I'm not going through all of this trouble just to make him angry. Him getting his hands on the data that is in that file, is literally a matter of life or death for some, and, like I said, it's worth billions. He's the last person on this planet that I wish would have access to that type of money."

Naomi couldn't help but start to pace in front of the two women. The more Genevieve revealed, the more questions Naomi had to ask. "Let's start from the beginning. How do you know what's in there when, I, the person who works on the server it's located on, didn't?"

Genevieve shrugged. "I would assume not many people know what's in that file either. I only know about it because Wilson and I had plans on stealing it together before he went 'rogue.' Since you didn't ask what was in it, I assume you now know that there is some data on some of the most high-profile people in the world, and a huge market for those who would want that information. Especially some of the darker and dirty things that are in the files."

Naomi debated about inquiring more about the details in the files but decided that wouldn't matter in the grand scheme of things. "So, with Morris kidnapping Paige and then later June, all of this was for me to break in and steal this data."

Molly nodded as Genevieve spoke. "That was the plan, and Morris took it a step too far. Now I'm sure he understands the consequences of his actions given his current place of residence."

Naomi doubted it but was willing to go along with whatever tale Genevieve was spinning. "If what you're saying is true, how do we get the evidence to prove Wilson is behind Sean's murder."

"Let me correct you by saying I don't think Wilson actually killed Sean. I do suspect he was the one, however, who called out the hit on Sean."

"He still needs to be held accountable, though."

"I'm not denying that. Anyway, my gut says he was paying Sean to try to do what Morris tried to get you to do, but Sean was digging somewhere he had no business digging, and he ended up being a loose end Wilson had to get rid of."

Naomi could see that being the case. "Going back to my original question, what evidence is there to paint this as being something Wilson did?"

"There isn't much, but I know he did it. The whole point of having someone else find the file and download its contents it's so that it would be hard to tie it back to him."

"So, Sean was doing all of his dirty work?"

"Yes, at least that was what he had envisioned when we were together. Not sure if that vision changed once we separated."

Naomi stopped pacing. "How does any of this involve me?"

"Morris had already been working for me for a while, and we knew you worked there. You must have done extremely well at your job, because I know Sean was put on the project because of his smarts, but also is ability to keep things quiet. Or so Wilson thought. I assume something happened or Wilson found out that he was about to betray him and that led to him ordering the hit." She took a deep breath before she continued. "I assume you were put on the server to do a job, whereas Sean was put on because Wilson wanted him on there and saw an opening with your appointment...at least that was the original idea he and I had. I used the fact that you were as a way to try to take the file right out from under Wilson's nose. It failed, as you very well know."

This information caused Naomi's mind to spin out of control. If the situation had been reversed, there was a good chance Naomi wouldn't be here right now because Wilson would've more than likely had her killed. "I assume you heard about Dwayne Clarence's death."

Genevieve nodded. "And, yes, before you ask, as far as I know the reason he was killed was because both Wilson and whoever it is that he's working for needed the uniform for the evening of Sean's murder."

"How'd you know I was going to ask that?"

Genevieve gave her a look that said 'really'? "MPD needs to do a better job of securing what they think is top secret."

Naomi made a note to pass along that information to them. "There has to be another catch with me coming here. Why tell me all of these things without me signing a contract in my blood?"

Genevieve smirked and looked at Molly. "I like her. Yes, there is something I want you to do for me. I want you to find a way to pin this back to Wilson and make sure he rots in jail or hell. Either one works for me."

"That's it?"

"Make sure the police don't know who I am. I'd prefer to… continue working under the radar. I know you're working for the police, but I get the sneaky suspicion you won't tell them a thing."

Naomi nodded. Something beeped, and Genevieve pulled out a phone from her pocket.

"Looks like we have a visitor." She turned the phone so

that Naomi could see, and Naomi wasn't shocked by who she saw on the other end. "Next time, if we meet again, hopefully you won't feel the need to have someone track you on your phone before you arrive."

"How'd you know—"

"I have my ways."

"So, the blindfold was just for shits and giggles?"

Genevieve shrugged, but a small smile played on her lips. "That was Molly's idea." She then turned to Molly. "Please show Naomi to the exit closest to where this camera is, so she can meet up with her boyfriend."

CHAPTER 21

"What are you doing here?" Naomi asked, causing Reed to swing around to look at her. She found him standing near an entrance to the parking garage she'd entered. Before she approached him, she'd taken a few seconds to look at her surroundings. She didn't recognize the area, but knew she was still in D.C.

"Paige called and told me that you left your apartment and asked her to track your movements. Seemed like a recipe for disaster, so I thought I would come here and try to save you from yourself."

Naomi almost snarled at him. "Stop being a dick, and you can leave now, because as you can see, I'm fine." She had just gotten hit with a ton of information that she was still trying to process. The last thing she needed was Reed's smart aleck remarks on top of everything she'd just learned. It seemed as if he was still pissed from the fight days before.

The anger in Naomi's voice must have registered because Reed took a step back with his hands up. "Listen, I was worried about you, and when Paige called, I didn't know what to think, especially after you haven't been answering my texts."

"There was a reason for that, wasn't there?"

"I know I could be handling this a lot better."

"We both could be. Look, I really need to go."

"That's fine. Do you want me to take you home?"

Naomi looked up and saw Reed's sedan parked a couple of spots from where they were standing. She knew this was probably his way of not only making sure she got home safely, but an opportunity for him to quiz her on where she'd gone.

"You should probably make a decision quickly. We don't know who is watching, including the person who tried to hit you with that dart."

If only Reed knew how true those words were. "Fine, you can take me home."

A small smile appeared on Reed's lips, and it was clear he thought he'd won this round. "I also have something to give to you," he said before he gestured for Naomi to walk to his car.

With an eyebrow raised, Naomi strolled to Reed's car, allowed him to open her car door, and slid inside the vehicle. Reed rounded the vehicle before he opened his door and settled into the driver seat. About a minute later, the couple were on the road toward Naomi's apartment.

Naomi glanced at her phone and saw she had several text messages from Paige.

Paige: Hey is everything okay?

Paige: Naomi?

Paige: I'm calling Reed to see if he can track you down. I'm worried sick.

Naomi: I'm so sorry I'm just now texting you back. I'm with Reed, and I'll be home shortly.

She hoped Paige wasn't going to be too upset with her and was now somewhat thankful she'd called Reed instead of the police. The last thing anyone needed to deal with was that.

"What was that about?"

Naomi decided to be obtuse. "What was all of what about?"

"What were you doing back there?"

"Following up on a lead. What is it that you had for me?"

"I've got permission to examine Sean's laptop."

"His Edmon laptop?"

Read nodded. "It looks as if Edmon did end up handing over Sean's laptop. MPD wasn't able to find anything, but I asked if we could check it out, because I knew you would know more about what he might have on the computer versus someone who is not familiar with Edmon."

"Thank you," was the only thing Naomi could say. Although she and Reed were on the outs right now, it didn't mean she couldn't express gratitude for what he had done.

"It might take me some time to go through everything, so I can call you tomorrow and tell you if I found something?"

"You were going to work on it tonight? It's pretty late."

"Eh, maybe? I'd see how I felt once I get home."

There was a lull in the conversation for a couple of minutes, and Naomi just enjoyed being back in Reed's presence for however brief it was. She enjoyed the quiet nights they spent together, and even if this car ride was a temporary return to what they had before their big fight, she'd take it.

"Are you going to tell me about the lead you were following up on?"

Naomi knew he wouldn't let up on it, and he was justified in that position. So, she answered in the best way she knew how. "I might know who killed Sean Barlow."

Read glanced at her at the corner of his eye. "And were you going to tell me?"

"Yes, I was. I was just trying to find out more information before I went accusing someone."

"Did Morris have anything to do with this?"

That wasn't a big jump. "He might've pointed me in a direction to find out who might have killed Sean, but I don't think he had anything to do with this."

"So, you did talk to him."

Reed's tone told her that he was making a statement versus a question, and she wondered if he was aiming to pick another fight. This was not a battle she was willing to have. "Reed, please, not right now." The words came out more pleadingly than she was wanted, but she hoped it got her point across.

"I'm just worried about you, okay? I've been thinking about it, and I wish I hadn't gotten you swept up in this case anyway."

"Why's that?"

"You're…I'm trying to find the right words for this, so bear with me. You're too connected to the case. And you're shutting me out of your life."

"Reed, I hardly think one fight means I'm shutting you out of my life. We've had disagreements before."

"Not like this. There's no doubt in my mind that had we not had that fight, and you went to talk to your father anyway, you would have told me about what was going before you took off in the middle of the night."

She couldn't deny that he was right. "I did more than talk to him. I rented a car to go see him."

Reed murmured something under his breath before

pinching lips as if he were trying to stop himself from saying something he might regret. "Did he have anything to do with why you're out and about this late?"

He looked at her as she nodded her head. This time, he let the colorful cusswords fly.

"Reed."

Her calling his name stopped the things that were flying out of his mouth in an instant. His eyes landed on her once again, and even with darkness all around them, she could see the love that shone in his eyes.

"How is your anxiety?"

Naomi wasn't sure how to answer that question. On one hand, she hadn't had an outright panic attack recently, but on the other hand, her stress and anxiety had been hovering at a level that made her think one could happen at any time. Still, she tried to push through it, and she knew she was doing so at a detriment to her mental health.

"I'm okay, I think, but there is a lot going on, so who really knows."

"Have you talked to Dr. Evans recently?"

"I have, but even with me talking to her, and doing breathing exercises and meditation and taking medication, it doesn't stop a panic attack sometimes. They can be unavoidable when your stress and anxiety get to a certain level, and I've learned to cope."

"I can understand that."

"But, as of now, I'm fine."

Reed placed his hand on her knee, causing a slight shiver to run through her body. "Good. I'm glad to hear it."

For the rest of the ride, Naomi expected him to talk more about her father's involvement and who she met with tonight, but he didn't. Instead, he just let the soft music that had been playing in the car when they started it be the only thing between them. His hand stayed on her knee, never straying up or down. She both appreciated it and was frustrated by it.

When he pulled up in front of her building, he made sure to put the car in park, making her wonder if he planned on staying for longer than she thought.

"Look, Naomi, I just want to apologize. I said what I said because I was concerned and thought you talking to your father would cause you greater turmoil, but I shouldn't have said that you shouldn't talk to him. I can't tell you what to do, and I was out of line."

"I knew what you were trying to do, and I know it was out of love and trying to protect me, but I am more than capable of making my own decisions."

"I know that. I understand that."

Naomi nodded her head and couldn't stop the yawn that left her mouth. Reed chuckled, and Naomi realized how much she missed that sound. How much she missed him.

"I'll walk you to your door, sleepy head."

Naomi shook her head and laughed. "You can come upstairs and spend the night, if you want."

"Are you sure?"

"I wouldn't have said it if I wasn't."

The smile on Reed's face could have lit up the entire car. "Okay, I like this plan."

He got out of the car, and Naomi followed. He quickly grabbed a bag she assumed had the laptop and walked with her through the lobby and toward the elevators in her apartment. Before Naomi even had a chance to unlock the door, it swung open, and a stressed-out Paige greeted the couple.

She immediately pulled Naomi into her arms, but just before she did, Naomi saw a look on her face that said that at the same time while she was relieved, she wanted to throttle her. "How are you? You promised to text me!"

"I know, I know. I'm sorry. I kind of couldn't."

"Can we take this inside before you wake up your neighbors?"

Both women glared at Reed who put his hands up in a mocking surrender. However, they did move, and Reed shut the door behind them.

"What happened?" Paige threw an arm around Naomi's shoulders and led her into the living room. Reed kept going to the kitchen, and Naomi and Paige sat down on their couch.

"I wasn't able to text you after a while. I'm so sorry. You probably thought I went missing…"

"Well, you kind of did, but I'm glad it wasn't the result of you being kidnapped." Reed walked back in with two cups of water before sitting down across from Naomi and Paige.

Naomi looked down at her hands, feeling guilty for having caused Paige to feel the way she did. Paige leaned over and hugged Naomi again.

When they pulled apart, Naomi said, "So I can't exactly go into detail about how I know this, or whether or not it's real, but arrows might be pointing to Wilson Billings being the person who ordered Sean and subsequently Dwayne's deaths."

Reed leaned forward waiting for Naomi to continue while Paige's mouth dropped open and her body flung back in surprise.

"You've got to be shitting me. Wilson is a huge donor to George's campaign. I've met him several times because of that."

That wasn't surprising to Naomi, since Edmon had a political action committee of its own, so Senator Butler and many other congressional members probably received thousands of dollars in donations.

"Just as we expected, whatever information is in Cyber Edge is worth a lot of money. Much more than Edmon is paying Wilson as CEO." Naomi reached forward and grabbed her water. She mouthed 'thank you' to Reed before taking a sip. Once she was done, she continued, "I think I mentioned this before, but I found it odd Wilson wanted Sean specifically to be on this project. Normally, it's a manager who decides who goes on what project. It makes no sense for Wilson to be so involved in that decision making, and no one who valued their job was going to deny him. That was a red flag for me."

"I saw the clips from the memorial. So, you're saying he stood up there and gave a speech about how wonderful Sean was, and he was the one who had him killed?"

Naomi nodded. "He was up there, waxing poetry about Sean, and I do believe he had him killed. The problem now is proving he did."

"Could something be on Sean's laptop? After all, how much security's on this thing."

Naomi looked up at Reed, wide eyed. "I would assume it has the same security features as mine, which it is pretty heavy duty given the work we are doing. I'm not sure if there are extra features on his computer that mine doesn't have." She glanced at the bag at Reed's feet before looking back up at him. "Looks like I have a long night ahead of me."

"Looks like *WE* have a long night ahead of us," Reed said as he stood up. "I'll make some coffee."

Paige stood up too. "Don't leave me out of this. I'm in, too."

CHAPTER 22

"**P**aige, why don't you go to sleep?"

"Because I'm trying to help." She stifled a yawn, which had to be the fifth one in the last ten minutes.

"It's okay. You don't need to sacrifice your sleep for this. I don't know when or if I'll find anything." Naomi rolled her neck to ease her muscles, smiling at Paige. She was so grateful to have such a supportive best friend in her life.

Paige stretched her arms up before tossing her blonde hair into a messy bun on the top of her head. "Will you tell me if you find something?"

"I will." *In the morning, once we've all gotten some sleep.*

"Okay, I'm going to bed. I'll see you both in the morning." Padding over, Paige gave Naomi a quick hug.

"Good night."

"Night," Reed chimed in from his spot on the couch next to Naomi. At some point during the evening, Paige and Reed had switched positions due to Paige's insistence that Reed sit next to Naomi. No one complained about it.

Paige gave a small wave, walking to her room without another word.

Reed looked over at Naomi. "How's the search going?"

"I don't know if I've ever seen so much shit on a computer in my life," Naomi said. She leaned back against the wall and closed her eyes, resting her weary mind for a moment. "You know what makes matters worse?"

"What?" Reed reached over and put his hand on her knee.

Feeling his touch on her bare skin because of the shorts she was wearing was an entirely different experience than when he touched her while driving her home.

"A lot of the things on his computer are in some sort of code. I'm not sure if this was just his process for tracking different tasks or if he was trying to hide something in case someone found it. All that to say is that it's giving me a headache." She gently massaged her temples.

"Why not take a break or get some sleep? We all could use some and then look at it with fresh eyes in the morning."

Naomi knew that Reed's point was a good one and maybe taking a step back and getting some rest would help her become more focused. "Fine."

Naomi stretched her arms over her head as Reed stood up. He held out his hand, offering to help her stand up. Naomi gazed at his hand before looking back up at him. The soft smile playing on his lips warmed her heart. That warmth soon spread throughout her whole body once she placed her hand within his and stood up, He helped her up and pulled her into his arms. His eyes studied her face before all of his focus was on her lips. He lifted her head slightly with his finger under her chin, before he cupped her face and leaned down to lay his lips on hers.

When they slowly pulled away, Reed rubbed his thumb along her jawline before he said, "Let's go to bed."

The couple walked into her room and once they were settled into bed, Naomi turned to him. "Wait, there's something I want to tell you."

"What's that?"

"I don't want there to be anything between us, so I want to tell you what happened tonight."

"Okay." Reed folded the pillow before plopping down on it. "Continue."

"I'm not supposed to tell the police this information."

"I'm not the police anymore."

Naomi raised an eyebrow.

"You'd be shocked to know some of the things I've gotten into while working a case as a private investigator."

Naomi shrugged, although she believed him. She then proceeded to tell him all about what had happened when she'd met Molly and Genevieve earlier that night. Once she was done, she looked at him with bated breath, wondering what his reaction would be.

"I don't know who Molly is, but most of the things you told me about Genevieve outside of anything related to Cyber Edge, I can confirm."

"Oh really?"

Reed nodded. "Genevieve Platt is Wilson's ex-wife, and there was a lot of contention with their divorce. From what I found in my research, it's pretty obvious they can't stand each other."

"What is it exactly that she does?" That question had been bothering Naomi ever since she'd left Molly and Genevieve.

"Real estate on the surface. What she does in her off time is up to interpretation but you got a first-hand glance into what she does."

"Going back to Wilson, you've been tracking Wilson this entire time?"

"No, I looked into him when I saw that he was everywhere as a result of Sean Barlow's murder. Not that he shouldn't be due to his position, but he gained a lot more favorability due to his leadership. Now, I can see your eyes drooping so it's time to go to sleep. We can talk more about this in the morning."

Naomi wasn't about to argue with him. Content to be back in Reed's arms, she drifted off to sleep, his hand rubbing up and down her back.

* * *

Naomi rounded the corner to her cubicle and sat down at her desk. Her fingers flew across the keyboard as she started her work day. She was focused on the code she was creating when she heard something drop to the floor. The noise was so loud that it caused her desk to

An object slowly entered her periphery, and she turned her body to get a better look at what it was. A bloody baseball slowly rolled to a stop near the entrance of the cubicle.

Naomi stood up slowly and walked to the ball. She looked up when she saw someone standing off to the side. Sean Barlow, dressed in dark jeans and a white button down, took one step toward her, but didn't say anything. Blood started dripping from his neck. His eyes were lifeless, unseeing, but fixed on her.

Naomi tried to scream, but no sound left her mouth. When he took another step toward her, she tried to turn and run, but tripped over the baseball. He continued his advance. She tried to crawl away, but something was holding her down. A flash of light ripped across her vision, and everything faded into white.

Naomi woke with a start. Darkness surrounded her as a familiar sensation was coming over her. She mentally begged it to stop. It felt as if her bedroom walls were closing in on her. A light sweat broke out over her skin as she looked over and found Reed sleeping just a few inches away from her. She debated waking him up, but didn't want to disturb his sleep.

Sleep. Naomi tried to force her mind to focus on it, but it was impossible. This couldn't be happening to her right now.

The pangs in Naomi's stomach were slowly growing stronger and there was almost nothing she could do to stop it. Her body's reaction to stress and anxiety was too far gone and her breathing exercises were rendered useless. The pain in her body picked up steam, causing her to maneuver into fetal position in hopes that it might stop the pain. She did her best not to make any noise.

Finding almost no relief from her new position, Naomi slowly made her way to the bathroom. She shivered as she grabbed the medication that might be her saving grace and quickly took the pill. Her shivers continued even though it was the middle of summer in Washington, D.C.

No matter how much she tried to gain control of the situation, her body continued to betray her as she waited for the medication to provide some relief, but it was slow coming. The pain grew in intensity as she leaned over her sink, trying to gain enough strength to walk back to bed. The stabbing feeling in her stomach made it difficult to think of anything else.

"Come on, work dammit," she murmured in between

heavy breathing as she waited for the pain to lessen. It didn't help that nausea was starting to kick in and she couldn't control the shivering of her body. Naomi couldn't determine what was sweat or tears as she tried to pull herself together.

"Naomi?"

She couldn't answer him, couldn't look at him. She felt like a failure for letting things get this bad again.

"What's wrong?" There was a pause before Reed said, "Anxiety attack?"

Naomi nodded her head slightly, not trusting herself to respond in case it might make the pain worse or cause her to throw up.

"Did you take anything for it?"

Another slight nod was the answer she gave.

"Can you make it back to bed with my help?"

She nodded, but she was unsure if she would be able to if she was being honest with herself. He walked over to her and slowly picked her up, deciding it was best for him to carry all of her weight, instead of just a piece of it.

He brought her over to her bed and tucked her in. "Stay there. Anything you need, I'll get for you." He bent down so they were eye level and wiped her tears. "You don't have to go through this alone. I'm going to grab some water and a washcloth for you and hopefully the medicine will start to ease the pain."

With that, he stood up and left her room. His words touched Naomi in a way she couldn't have predicted. More tears fell from her eyes that had nothing to do with the pain she was feeling, but due to how much his words had just rocked her world.

Reed was back with a glass of water and a warm compress

within a couple of minutes. When he placed the washcloth on her head and a glass of water within arm's reach on her night stand, he turned back to her and asked, "Are you feeling any better?"

"Yeah, I think the medicine is finally kicking in so I'll hopefully be back on my feet soon. Thanks for...well everything," Naomi said with a sad smile. She hadn't planned on falling apart in front of him like this especially when they had just gotten over a big disagreement.

"Of course. I'd do anything to help you feel better." He brushed away the last tear that was slowly making its way down her face before he walked over to his side of the bed and laid next to her.

Naomi could feel her body calming down. Based on past experience, she knew it would be several hours before she felt as if she was back to her normal self, but just having her body feel as if it were attacking itself was a step in the right direction. The medicine she took was making her feel a little drowsy, so she turned over and faced Reed as she tried to get comfortable on her other side.

Her eyelids felt heavy, but she watched Reed as he studied her. He placed a piece of her dark curly hair behind her ear before he pulled her toward him, so she could rest her head on his chest. The steady beat of his heart was all she heard as she fell into a dreamless sleep.

CHAPTER 23

Naomi awoke and looked out of her window. The bright sunshine told her it had to be late morning, or early afternoon. She still felt a bit weak after her anxiety attack in the early morning hours, but she no longer felt that stabbing pain or shivers that had coursed through her body just hours before. She looked toward the other side of the bed and didn't find Reed. Had he gone home? If so, she wouldn't blame him after the attack she'd last night or maybe that was her anxiety talking.

Naomi slowly took the covers off her body and eased out of bed, not trusting that any of the symptoms she had experienced wouldn't return. Once she was confident that her body seemed to be behaving how it usually did, she walked out of her room and toward the living room.

There, she spotted Reed sitting on her couch with Sean's laptop in his lap.

"Hey," she said, her voice just above a whisper as she made her way over to him.

"Hey yourself. Is there anything I can get you?"

Naomi shook her head as she sat down and he pulled her into his side.

"Paige told me to tell you that she was going to be running some errands, but that she'd be back soon."

"Okay. Did you find anything on Sean's computer?"

"No. I thought I would at least try while you were resting to see if something would pop, but so far nothing has. You were right about the state of his computer. So many files and the way his things are organized…he certainly had a system it seems only he could decipher."

Naomi didn't respond, instead choosing to close her eyes while resting her head on Reed's shoulder. She was feeling more and more like herself thankfully. After about a minute, she sat up. An idea popped into her head. "Do you think that was done by design?"

"It could be. It could just be the way he liked to organize his work files."

"Or he was trying to hide something in plain sight. After all, if I knew I would be working on the server that contained files like Cyber Edge, I'd have backups of my backups."

"What if Sean did? Doug and I both have external hard drives that saves our data. Did anyone at MPD find any hard drives when they dug through Sean's things?"

"I could double check with Finley."

Naomi clapped her hands and pointed at Reed. "Shit! He could have even backed it up to the cloud. Whether it was on his own server or on Edmon's…what if the answer has been under our noses the entire time!" Naomi jumped but immediately regretted it because her head hurt once she was standing.

"Wait, slow down, tiger. I'm not following you completely." His brow furrowed as he tried to follow her train of thought.

"Reed, what if Sean kept some record of the conversations he was having with Wilson, if he is indeed the person behind all of this, as insurance of sorts? We need to find it because that might be the only way we can find out who was responsible for his and Dwayne's murders."

"Okay, let's do it."

"Wait, I need to keep working on his computer here and see if it's on his computer somewhere. If it's not, and MPD didn't find anything at his home or in the office, we'll more than likely have to go to the office if it's indeed there."

"Wait, you mean you can't access it remotely?"

Naomi shook her head. "If I had to guess where he put it based on where I also have access, it can only be done on site and in a secure location."

Reed digested the information that Naomi told him. "Looks like we have work to do."

Naomi went into her room to grab her laptop, turning it on as soon as she was seated next to Reed.

Afternoon turned to evening as Naomi painstakingly tried to find any files that might connect Sean to Wilson or to anyone else who might have benefited from him being on the project. After taking several breaks for necessities such as food and due to still being tired from the anxiety attack that she'd had hours ago, Naomi closed Sean's laptop and put it on the coffee table. She placed her hands over her face and groaned.

"Nothing huh?" Reed asked.

"Nothing. In my opinion, if the reason why Sean was killed was due to Cyber Edge, there is no way that there isn't some form of a paper trail that could be accessed from his computer."

"Or Genevieve is lying."

"Could be that as well."

"Outside of any communication that could've happened on the server, it is possible that plans about the murder happened in person or through a private messenger? There are plenty of texting apps that encrypt messages." Reed's suggestion possibly confirmed Naomi's worst suspicions.

"I know I was just hoping that wasn't one of them. That makes things even harder." She groaned in frustration.

"There is something we can do."

Naomi perked up. "What?"

"Let's go find Wilson Billings." Reed looked at his watch and said, "I'm willing to bet he's at home."

Naomi grabbed Reed's arm. "Wait a minute. We can't just stalk him."

"I like to think of it as gathering information about a person but you can use whatever term you would like. We're just going to sit out in my car and follow him if he leaves."

"Reed, this is my job. If I get found stalking the CEO of my company, I'm getting fired."

"Not if we can help it. Make sure you have everything you need to get into Edmon…just in case we need to stop by there as well."

"I can do that." Naomi clapped her hands again. "This is my first stake out. How exciting! But first I should shower."

She could see that Reed was fighting to keep from laughing. "I'm going to send a couple of messages and then I'll join you."

* * *

As Naomi fixed the dark green t-shirt that she'd just put on, she heard Reed talking on the phone. She was disappointed he never joined her in the shower, but she understood that he was busy trying to solve the case. When she walked into her bedroom, she spotted Detective Finley on his phone. She waved at him since Reed had him on video chat before walking over to her dresser. Just as Naomi was about to grab her brush to put her hair into a ponytail, Reed spoke.

"Oh, here she is. Maybe she can confirm it right now."

Since it was clear Reed had been talking about her while she was in the shower, she walked over to him and asked, "Confirm what right now?"

"Have you ever been to Wilson's office?"

"Yes, of course. We met there when I reported to him about this server. Why?"

"Does this look like his office at Edmon to you?" This time, it was Detective Finley who spoke. A picture of an office flashed on the screen.

Naomi recognized it immediately. "Things are somewhat different from the last time I was in there, but it looks like his office at Edmon."

"I think we have our answer."

Reed nodded his head in agreement and Naomi was left looking puzzled in front of the two men.

"What are you talking about?"

"I'll explain in the car. We need to go. Thanks, Finley."

"Don't mention it. Let us know what you find." Reed hung up the phone and turned to Naomi. "We should head out."

Naomi grabbed the things she needed and both she and Reed were soon on their way to Wilson's home.

"You never made it to the shower, who all did you call?"

"Some old contacts of mine that I asked to help me gather research on Wilson a couple of days ago. So, I figured I'd reach out to them again just in case they had any more information."

"That's smart. Makes sense."

Reed parked about a half a block up from Wilson Billings' house, which was located in the Chevy Chase neighborhood in Washington, D.C. The big, beautiful estate boasted six bedrooms, seven bathrooms, including a pool that was probably the size of Naomi's apartment.

"What is it we're waiting for?" Naomi asked.

"We're waiting to see if Wilson leaves to go to the Edmon offices at any point tonight."

"Wait, why would he do that?"

"Heard from a confidante that Wilson has been going to Edmon in the evenings since Sean's death."

"Really? Any idea why?"

"At least, on the surface, he's been going there to have meetings and interviews with different media organizations to discuss the steps Edmon is taking to make sure that this doesn't happen again."

Naomi's head swerved to look at Reed. "He's going all the way to Edmon to do interviews?" She pointed to his house. "He has plenty of space in that house to be conducting them there."

Reed looked over at her with a pointed stare. "Exactly. Why would someone travel all the way to their office, multiple times a week, when most of the staff is working from home during off hours just to do interviews and meetings when he easily has access to those things at home?"

"Strange, you couldn't pay me to leave my house after hours to go back into work. It would be different if I was still there during the course of the day."

"Most people wouldn't, so what is he doing there after hours?" Reed turned his attention back toward Wilson's house.

Naomi worried her lower lip between her teeth. "I don't know, but I hope we find out soon."

CHAPTER 24

"I think I see movement at his house."

Naomi turned to look at Reed before looking back at the house. From her vantage point, she could see car headlights heading down Wilson's driveway toward the street Her heart rate picked up speed as the car paused before turning onto the street.

"Duck down when he gets closer to our car," Reed ordered.

Naomi wanted to get a head start on his instructions so she slid down in her seat so that it would be hard for anyone to see who she was. When the SUV passed by the vehicle, Reed shot up in his seat and waited a beat before starting his car. She assumed he did that to further avoid another possible way to alert Wilson to what they were doing.

"I couldn't see if there's anyone else in the car, but I'm pretty sure I saw Wilson driving," said Reed.

Before Naomi could say anything, he pulled away from the curb and followed Wilson down the street. Thankfully, during the time it took for Reed to drive off, another car passed them, putting another barrier between their car and Wilson's.

Naomi hoped it would be enough for Wilson to not get suspicious.

"Do you do this often?"

Reed glanced at her, but his attention was mostly focused on keeping an eye on Wilson and on the road. "Do I do what?"

"Sit outside people's houses and watch them, looking for anything they might be partaking in to build up a profile for them."

"Sometimes. This job ebbs and flows. You never know what you're going to get into on any given day."

"That must make it exciting and more adventurous than sitting in front of a monitor all day."

"You could say that."

Naomi stared at him. "What would you call it then?"

"All part of a day's work."

Naomi rolled her eyes and turned her focus back to Wilson's SUV. As they drove down the streets of D.C., she started recognizing some of the sights. "He's definitely going to Edmon."

"Just in time for some of the late-night television shows. Probably more interviews that will help his popularity," Reed snorted derisively.

Nerves leapt through Naomi's body. "Do we have some kind of plan to catch him if he is trying to steal Cyber Edge? How are we going to catch him?"

"Well, it depends."

"Depends on what?" Mild frustration seeped into Naomi's tone. Reed couldn't leave her hanging right there.

"I want to answer your question with a question which will then answer your question. Does that make sense?"

She narrowed her eyes. "Yes. Continue."

"Does the server that contains the Cyber Edge file keep a record of who might be accessing or trying to access the data?"

"Yes, we all have IP addresses and an ID number which is our unique code. I'm sure a lot of the things we have access to at Edmon keep track of who is accessing it and when and where. I would imagine it's even more stringent for that server."

"Then I have a good enough plan that I think will help us nab Wilson if he's trying to access the server to find the Cyber Edge file, if that is indeed what he is going after."

"Speaking of that, you haven't asked me a pretty important question."

Reed raised an eyebrow at her. "What's that?"

"I'll explain. Normally, when someone is trying to access a file, it is pretty easy to just take it from your hard drive or a server and move it or copy it to wherever you want to place it, and then go about your day. This hasn't been the case with Wilson, if he is doing what we think he's doing. This has been a several days long project, not counting when he had Sean doing his dirty work."

Naomi watched as Reed processed what she'd said. His eyes widened briefly as the pieces fell into place. "I'm such an idiot."

"No, you're not. I should've explained what I'd found out before, but honestly with everything going on, it took me a second to connect the dots." Naomi took a deep breath. "After everything that went down with Morris, I did a little research myself. It seems as if Cyber Edge is not called Cyber Edge on the server. Even if you were able to get past all of the security protocols, you would still have to search for the actual file. And there are who knows how many files on that server. Could be millions or billions, for all we know."

"The search is taking so long because Wilson doesn't know where it is. It's essentially like finding a needle in a haystack… is that the old saying?"

Naomi chuckled. "That is an old saying and that's exactly what this is like. If this is what he's doing now and he killed Sean for whatever reason, his search is probably taking him even longer unless he has someone else working alongside him, helping him. Sean was probably trying to create a script that would make it easier to find the file and give it to Wilson."

"Wilson pretty much screwed himself over."

Naomi agreed. "He's in too deep now. I have to find that file. Who knows who he promised it to. Also, this leaves the question of why Wilson would kill his best chance of uncovering the file quickly."

"I could only assume he knew something he shouldn't have, and Wilson wasn't having it," Reed aptly concluded.

Naomi pointed up the street. "There's a parking spot. We can walk over to Edmon from there."

Reed swung into the parking spot and turned off the car. The couple exited the car and Reed went into the backseat and grabbed both Sean's and Naomi's laptops. The two walked side by side near to the corner of the block the building was on before Naomi gestured for Reed to follow her down another block.

"Where are we going?" Confusion marred his features.

Naomi smiled mischievously. "To enter the building from another entrance that only Edmon employees have access to.

Just in case anyone is waiting to attack. I don't want either of us getting hurt or worse if we can avoid it."

"I like the way you think." He grinned at her with approval.

"Why thank you, Mr. Wright."

"Maybe being a PI is something you should consider in the future" he said sincerely.

"I've been a software developer since I joined the workforce."

"Doesn't mean you can't use your skills elsewhere.

Naomi paused for half a beat to look at Reed, before continuing on. She walked up to the entrance and flashed her badge that was on her phone over the scanner. The door opened with a light beep, and Naomi and Reed walked in.

We should set up at your desk. I assume we can watch if he accesses it from there."

Naomi nodded, answering Reed without saying a word.

They walked over to the elevator, and Reed reached over and pressed the button. In no time at all, they were exiting onto the floor where Naomi worked.

Fixing on a lamp Naomi had recently bought for her desk, she logged into the server. "Here we are," she mumbled.

Reed leaned over her shoulder. "Can you see anyone on the server yet?"

Naomi smiled at his enthusiasm. "Patience."

Reed leaned against her desk with his feet and arms crossed. It seemed as if they would be there for the long haul. Naomi was about to get up and pace when she noticed something on her monitor that made her sit back down in her chair with a thump.

"What's wrong? What do you see?"

"Someone just modified a file on to the server. I can see it right there." It was faster than she had expected, but not surprising considering how many nights Wilson had probably been spending searching for the elusive file. He wasn't liable to waste any time.

Reed moved back to his position standing over her shoulder and Naomi clicked on the window that would bring up the list of documents. She knew which one was her IP address, so she quickly flipped over to Edmon's virtual directory. After a few clicks, she typed in the number and waited for the person's information to appear on the screen.

"It's him. It's fucking—"

Before she could finish her thought, the lamp turned off and her computer flickered as it switched to running on battery power. She closed it to prevent the light from shining in the room.

She slowly rose out of her chair and reached for Reed. Naomi could feel Reed's breath on her ear as he whispered, "Someone cut the electricity and we need to get you out of here as soon as possible."

Naomi knew it was dangerous coming in here to this. Wilson would have been able to do the exact same thing she'd done and saw her on the server. It wouldn't take the smartest person in the world to figure out what Wilson nor Naomi were doing at this time of night, in the Edmon building, especially after the warning she'd been served by Doug.

She heard Reed moving in the darkness, but she couldn't see him all that well. Although there was a faint light shining in from the street lights down below, it wasn't high or bright enough to light up the space. The urge to pull out her phone and use it as a flashlight was there, but she didn't want to draw more attention to her or Reed. And it was clear that Wilson knew where they were.

Naomi was afraid to whisper, because she didn't know how close Wilson was to them. At least they didn't know until the lights suddenly turned back on. It seemed as if every single light in the room full of cubicles were flicked on quickly, casting a bright light around the room. It took both Naomi and Reed squinted as they adjusted to the new source of light and when Naomi could finally see, she saw a dart whizzing toward her face.

Without a word, Reed dragged her down to the ground with him, narrowly helping Naomi avoid getting hit by the dart.

CHAPTER 25

"Did you enjoy our little light show? I thought you might want to join the after-hours party when I saw you on the server."

Naomi put her hands up, casting a sidelong glance to see if Reed had followed suit.

"You couldn't just back off like Clint here warned Doug, but you didn't. How much more patient can a man be?"

Reed moved to pull Naomi behind him, protecting her from possible harm. However, she jumped when a throat cleared behind them. Wilson's bodyguard from the Sean Barlow memorial was standing there, playing with a knife. Reed adjusted his body, in an attempt to block her from both sources of danger. "So you sent your bodyguard to do your dirty work and kill Sean Barlow."

Although Naomi's heart was pounding, she felt even more disgusted than she thought by the situation. "You're the bodyguard we saw guarding the door while Wilson spoke at the memorial. You had the nerve to kill him and then stand there like you didn't have anything to do with it. The one who said there was no one behind the curtain just before Wilson was speaking."

"Very good." Wilson slowly clapped, sarcasm dripping off of every world.

"How could you have no problem stealing data that Edmon is supposed to be protecting? You literally turned your back on who knows how many people including the employees who put in the work every day to make sure that this company keeps turning a profit and providing a service for the general public. This goes against everything that Edmon is supposed to stand for, and you do it with a smile on your face." Naomi edged out from behind Reed, furious at Wilson.

Wilson shrugged. "Sometimes, my dear, there are much higher powers at play. And money talks."

"What I don't know is why? Why kill the only person who could possibly help you find Cyber Edge or whatever other file you wanted on the server?" Naomi jabbed her finger toward her monitor for emphasis.

"Because I found out that he was getting ready to go to the police with all of the evidence showing I was trying to steal it. Couldn't have that happen, of course."

Naomi could hear the thinly veiled threat in his tone. "So, you decided it was better to eliminate the only person who could help you get that file?"

A sickly smirk appeared on his face. "No, I didn't." His stare made Naomi's heart pound faster. "You're going to sit down in that chair and find the Cyber Edge file. No one else is capable, and I assume you won't be as foolish as Sean." The words Naomi had dreaded to hear slipped out. How had she gotten herself into this situation again?

Even if she had the ability to find the file right away, there was no way she was giving it over to him. "And if I refuse?"

"You watch as your boyfriend gets the same treatment that Sean received."

Naomi gulped. Of course, she didn't want to see Reed in any pain but based on how shook he was when he came back from Sean's murder scene, she could imagine that she didn't want to see Reed that way. Heck, just the description of it caused her to have a very vivid nightmare that led to an anxiety attack.

"I have no problem trying to write a code that will help achieve this. I don't know how successful this will be, but–"

"Sit down and get to work, Naomi." Wilson's tone was cold and menacing.

Naomi glared, sick of people trying to tell her what she should and shouldn't do. "Absolutely not. Even if I did, it could take days before I had any results."

"I have time, plenty of time." A sneer parted his lips.

Wilson took a step toward them, and Reed said, "Back up, motherfucker."

Reed's words drew the attention of Wilson. He tilted his head. "Does she know why you quit the force?"

When Reed didn't say anything right away, Wilson smiled and took another step toward the couple.

"Boss, I have your knife."

Out of the corner of her eye, Naomi watched his body-guard advancing on them too as the light glinting off the blade of his knife. Someone needed to act, and it needed to be quick.

As if hearing the words that were playing in her head, Naomi ducked as Reed did, and before she could figure out where he'd gone, she looked up and found Reed pointing a gun at Wilson.

"You know I expected you to turn the gun on Clint there."

"Why would I do that? You probably couldn't care less whether or not Clint dies."

Reed had made a great deduction under a lot of stress. With Naomi still bending down on the ground, she pressed a button, signaling the police from her phone, yet muting the noise so no one in the room would know what she had done. She'd hoped maybe they'd even have someone patrolling the area right now, due to the spotlight Edmon was under right now. She quickly put her phone back in her pocket.

"There's one thing I want to know. How did you become suspicious of me?"

Naomi put her hands back up and tried to look as innocent as possible as she returned to a standing position. She could feel Wilson shuffled behind Reed, satisfied that she had nothing else in her hand.

"You were the one who was everywhere after Sean's death. All the interviews and press conferences seemed like overkill although the messaging was almost perfect. That alone wouldn't have meant as much, but it was enough to start digging. Then there's the fact that your ex-wife openly admitted to whatever plan you had to take the Cyber Edge file, while you were married." Naomi watched as Wilson's face switched from a smarmy, confident smile to one filled with hatred and rage.

"Of course, Genevieve would have said something. She has been out to get me ever since I asked for a divorce."

Naomi couldn't help but think that these two people were perfect for one another in a demented way, however, admitting that out loud might draw fire from Wilson. After all, he was still holding the high-powered dart gun.

"There's something I want to know as well."

All of the men in the room turned to face Naomi, who still stood with your hands up. "Why did you choose me to be on a server with the Cyber Edge file?"

"We honestly needed the best of the best on it and I had several managers at Edmon compile information on their whole team of developers and we chose you and Sean. Little did I know that my sweet ex-wife would have roped you into attempting to deliver the data in the Cyber Edge file to her. I also never would have thought you'd condoned your biological father's actions enough to even try to steal it."

Naomi glared. "Don't put words in my mouth. I don't condone the actions that any of them took to get what they wanted. You had no problem having members of your staff injured and murdered, all for what? A file that no one can find? I haven't even brought up Dwayne Clearance from Technological Mechanics."

Wilson raised his eyebrow. "You found out about him?"

"We did, and I wonder if there are any more victims out there."

Wilson stared right through her and Naomi knew that he wasn't use to having anyone tell him what he was going and wasn't going to do.

"Get to work, Naomi."

"No, I'm not—"

"You don't have a choice here, and this is non-negotiable!"

Naomi could see the rage building from within him. He

raised his dart gun and stalked toward them, and Reed adjusted his position, finger trained on the trigger. "If you get any closer, I'm willing to take the chance that either a dart from that gun hits me or your bodyguard here attempts to stab me. But all of those options mean that there will be a bullet in your skull."

"Clint should have killed you when he had the opportunity outside of Barry Stein's house. Then none of this would have come to light. But that's okay, because we have an opportunity to correct this now. Do you know why Clint likes killing with knives?"

Naomi shook her head, hoping that she was buying some more time.

Wilson gestured for Clint to speak. "Because it makes the kill more personal. You have to get up close to get the job done. And I can't wait to show you." He licked his lips, grinning wildly.

Wilson took another step toward her. Between his words and actions, Naomi couldn't help but to step back, but Reed remained firm. She wished that she and Reed could talk over a plan of attack, but there was no way they could in their current state.

Naomi retreated further and the backs of her thighs hit her desk. *Was there anything on her desk that she could grab quickly and use as a weapon? Where were the cops?*

She moved her hands slightly and came into contact with her stapler and an idea formed in her mind about what they could do. But how could she communicate her idea to Reed?

Naomi pulled the stapler around and tapped it on Reed's thigh. Thankfully the walls of the cubicle were high enough that neither man on the other side of the wall were any wiser. Reed nodded and Naomi tapped his thigh once, then twice, and when she tapped it three times, she chucked the stapler at Clint's head.

Her aim was off by a smidge but it did enough to distract him and he ducked to get out of the way. That gave Reed enough time to shoot Wilson and he turned to Naomi and yelled, "Run!"

Instead of running out of the cubicle where she would have met either man who was determined to kill her, Naomi climbed over the cubicle wall, on the desk and down to the floor before she took off running. Her exercise routine proved to be her best asset because she sprinted toward the exit. The only thing Naomi could hear was her heart thrashing in her ears, she knew that this was the best option they had to make it out of this alive. Fear propelled Naomi forward as her feet took her away from the danger and she hoped that Reed would be okay when she got back.

As if something heard her pray, the elevator doors burst open and she almost ran into Detective Finley. "They're in there!" Naomi screamed. Most of the MPD officers charged forward while one officer stayed back with Naomi.

"Are you okay, ma'am?"

Naomi nodded and wiped her face. Tears must have started falling from her eyes while she was running and she was too busy trying to run away to notice.

"We're going to go downstairs."

Naomi did a double take. "Why?" She didn't want to leave without Reed.

"For your safety, we need to exit the building."

Naomi didn't want to argue and followed the officer as he led her further and further away from the room.

She could hear shouting coming from the room and she hoped that meant that the officers were subduing both Wilson and Clint. What concerned her was that she hadn't seen Reed exited the room yet. She stared behind her as she hoped Reed would emerge from the room while she was still on that floor, but he didn't.

Time went by at a glacial pace as Naomi stood outside of her office building, wondering what was going on with the love of her life. She'd hoped by now that he would have joined her, yet she was still waiting outside with these emergency personnel all alone.

She'd already asked one of the police officers that she was standing near, if they'd heard anything but all he did was shake his head. So, she had no choice but to wait anxiously for news.

When paramedics raced into the building, Naomi's heart started beating wildly. She hoped that Reed wasn't seriously injured nor did he need medical attention. She didn't know how much time had passed, but when there was a commotion coming from the lobby, she held her breath as she waited for news about whether Reed was okay or not.

The first to exit were Wilson and Clint, both in handcuffs and Wilson was sporting a bandage on his arm. A few more seconds passed before she saw the person that filled her life with so much love and joy. Her heart skipped a beat and she almost cried from happiness as she watched Reed search the crowd that had formed to find her. She jogged toward him when he spotted her and the smile on his face mirrored her own.

"You're okay," she exclaimed just before he picked her up off of the ground.

"Of course I am. You can't get rid of me that easily."

He then planted a kiss on her lips, one she'd hoped would never end.

CHAPTER 26

Naomi sat outside of the office nervously jiggling her leg as she waited to be called. She wanted to get this over as soon as possible.

"Naomi?"

Naomi looked up and found Lynn Tucker, the Vice President of Edmon, standing in front of her. She slightly nodded her head as she stood up, ready to get this over with. Naomi brushed her hands down her slacks in an attempt to remove any of the clamminess that had developed as she waited for her name to be called.

"Come in," she said as Naomi walked into the office and Lynn closed the door behind her. When Naomi was settled in the chair in front of the desk, Lynn walked around her desk and sat down before she asked, "What can I do for you today?"

Naomi took a deep breath and said, "I'd like to hand in my resignation today."

Lynn nodded her head. "We're going to miss you and the work that you've done for Edmon has been nothing short of remarkable."

Naomi gave a small smile, appreciating the compliment. "Edmon has given me a lot over the years including helping me grow in a career that I love. But I think now's a great time to take a step back and explore new things and adventures."

It had been three weeks since she and Reed had taken Wilson Billings down, and the media attention had been overwhelming. She hadn't been back to work since because she couldn't see herself working for Edmon ever again.

This didn't mean that she didn't like her coworkers. Doug has been a great boss and mentor and grabbing lunch or coffee with June had been just a couple of the highlights of her to wear an Edmon. Telling them that she was leaving was going to be one of the hardest things she ever had to do. But the company itself was tainted to her.

"If I can be honest, given everything that has happened, I don't blame you."

Naomi chuckled. This entire year at Edmon had been non-stop drama, yet she still felt weary venturing out into the unknown.

"We can talk about the specifics of your resignation and figure out how this all will unfold and get human resources involved."

Naomi smiled. A weight had been lifted off her shoulders and she felt almost free.

* * *

MORRIS,

Thank you for leading us to the person who killed Sean Barlow. Although I can't speak for his family, I would think that they are happy that the murderer is behind bars. You are right, there are plenty of questions that I have left unanswered and I would like to talk about those as well for me to try to recover from the trauma that you have caused in my life. This is not a slight at you, I'm sure we both understand why this whole experience has been traumatic for me over the years.

Once again, thank you on behalf of everyone that was connected with this case,

N.

When she pressed send, she breathed a sigh of relief. Morris had kept his distance since she visited him, but she still felt the need to write this letter. It wasn't for him, it was for herself, finally taking the opportunity that was given to her to relieve some of the burden she carried from his abandonment. The few words that she typed on the page were only a small part of how she felt about him and what he'd done.

"This is just what we needed."

Naomi looked up from her phone and gave Reed a beaming smile. "I completely agree. How did you decide on us going to Puerto Rico?"

Reed smiled before he brushed a curl from her face. "I remember seeing how happy you were in that photo with you, Jada, and Logan in Puerto Rico after your college graduation, I believe?"

Naomi nodded.

"I hoped after everything that happened, coming here would be a great opportunity to relax and create some new memories."

And they had. Reed and Naomi had enjoyed some of the sights that Puerto Rico had to offer. They visited Old San

Juan, hiked through El Yunque National Forest, and tried a bunch of delicious foods.

Right now, they were lounging by their own personal pool at the home that they'd rented out for the week to recharge.

Naomi looked into Reed's sparkling blue eyes and couldn't help but bask in the warmth of his love. Just knowing how much he cared, no matter the issue, meant everything to her. And for him to plan out this whole trip based off of a picture he saw on her dresser months ago, made her heart sing. "That's so sweet of you."

When he leant down to kiss her, Naomi didn't shy away from kissing the love of her life. Their kiss helped Naomi feel at peace, peace with the decisions she'd made and happy to at least have the next week or so in paradise, soaking up the sun and enjoying time away from any drama in Washington, D.C.

"It was also an excuse to see you in a bikini."

Naomi rolled her eyes and lightly shoved him. She adjusted the hot pink bikini top she'd decided to wear today. "And here I was going to say there's no one I would rather be here with than you."

Reed smirked. "I'm happy to know that because you're stuck with me in more ways than one."

Naomi knew he was referring to the fact that she'd left her job just a couple of weeks prior and was now technically unemployed. "Fine."

"Fine what?"

"I'll join your PI business. Not sure what role I'll play, but it will be exciting to work together."

Reed looked like a kid in a candy store. "I can't wait to teach you everything I know."

"That makes me a little scared."

There was nothing that could be done to wipe the smile off of his face. "You *really* are stuck with me."

Naomi grabbed a hold of his swim trunks and pulled him toward her. "And I wouldn't have it any other way."

This time, Naomi's lips crashed into his, telling him everything he needed to know about where this was going. She opened her mouth slightly, allowing his tongue to enter. That began the dueling match that wouldn't declare a victor.

His arms came around her body, engulfing her and pulling her closer to him. His hands landed on her back as his fingertips left a trail of fire as they made their way down toward her ass. When he reached her bottom, he pulled away from the kiss, before catching her bottom lip lightly between his teeth.

"Jump and put your legs around my waist," he said once he let go of her lip.

"You just want to grab my ass."

"False. I want to carry you back into the villa. Grabbing your ass is the cherry on top of this hot sundae."

Naomi laughed. "I swear there's a thing about you and desserts…" She did as he asked with his help. He carried her back into their property they were staying on while in Puerto Rico and gently tossed her on the first bed he found.

Naomi couldn't help but giggle as Reed joined her. He crawled over her and laid another kiss on her lips, this one with even more fury than the one near the pool. She felt his hands shift to the back of her neck, where he made quick work of the bikini top she was wearing.

His eyes zeroed in on the present he had unwrapped and his mouth began to lick and suck on her exposed nipple. His other hand made its way to her other breasts, making sure to give it the attention it deserved.

Naomi's moans as her body tried to get even closer to him, craving the way he made her feel at this very moment. Her hands alternated between playing with his dark brown hair and falling down by her sides and clenching the sheets underneath her hands.

Somehow, he removed both her bikini bottoms and his swim trunks within seconds of each other and soon they were touching one another everywhere, driving each other into madness. When he sunk himself into her, she groaned.

"I want it fast."

"Oh really? What if I just teased you like this?" He slowly moved his hips and she could have throttled him if given the opportunity.

"So help me—"

Suddenly he started moving faster, just like she demanded and it took her by surprise. When she watched the smirk form on his face, she wanted to throttle him but he was driving her closer and closer to ecstasy. When she reached her release, she cried out in glee, but he wasn't done yet.

"I know you could do it again." His pace never slowed. "Come on, baby."

She looked at him wide eyed, but when he filled her up again and again, she believed that could. Soon she was crashing over the edge once more and this time he joined her.

What could be better than making love in paradise?

Stay tuned for a sneak peek of Behind the Scandal!

"Dinner was fantastic, Nana."

"I'm so glad you enjoyed it," Angie replied. She stood up and started clearing the plates.

Naomi jumped up and said, "Why don't Reed and I clear up in here and you and Irene go relax and watch some television?"

The two older women looked at each other and smiled. "You don't have to tell me twice," said Irene.

Naomi and Reed had gone over to Angie's house after she invited them and Irene over for dinner on a warm summer's night. It had been a while since they'd gotten together and Reed and Naomi now made it a point to visit both of their grandmothers as often as possible. The last few weeks had made things a bit harder, but the couple wanted to make sure that both women knew that it was a priority. Their grandmas stood up and left, leaving the dishes behind for their grandchildren.

Reed waved his hand over the faucet, turning it on and

Naomi continued to bring dishes toward the sink. When she picked up the remaining dishes, she turned around and felt small droplets of water on her face. "Did you just spray me with water?"

"Maybe I did?"

"Doesn't Angie have a Simon? You don't even need to do dishes. You didn't even have to turn the faucet on. You flicked water at me on purpose."

Reed shrugged. "What are you going to do about it?"

"This!"

Naomi darted over to the sink and wet her hands before for flicking the water at Reed. He didn't stop her, although he could have and their "water fight" turned into a laugh fest between the couple.

Just as they were trying to catch their breaths, Naomi's phone rang. She glanced down and saw that it was her best friend and roommate, Paige.

"Hey, what's up?"

"Naomi, I need you to get over here right now."

"What—what's wrong?" Naomi leaned on the kitchen counter.

"You need to get down here now. Bring Reed too."

"Paige, slow down where are we going?"

"Capitol Hill."

That made Naomi stand up straighter. "What happened?"

"Just come down here to my office."

With that, Paige hung up and Naomi was left staring at the phone. What the heck had gotten into Paige?

"You look as if you saw a ghost."

"I feel as if I have…" She stood up and looked at Reed. "We

might have another case and somehow, Paige is connected to this one as well."

* * *

Pre-order Behind the Scandal Today!

ABOUT THE AUTHOR

B. Ivy Woods has been writing for as long as she can remember. After getting her Bachelor of Arts in Political Science and Environmental Policy and a Master's in Energy Policy and Law and working in the environmental field for several years, she decided to become a stay-at-home mom. That is when thoughts of a writing career really took off. Although she competed in NaNoWriMo multiple times, 2019 was the first year that she won. This win inspired her to make writing a career. Her debut novel was self-published in 2020.

Although she is originally from New York City, she currently lives in the DMV (Washington, D.C., Maryland, Virginia) with her husband, daughter, dog, and cat.

www.bivywoods.com

9 781735 283685